SURPRISE ATTACK

Already, it was too late for Roarke. The terrorist saw the first figure swerve, come up clutching a weapon in target acquisition.

The Sandman was about to put him to sleep the hard way.

Frantically, he scrabbled for the Soviet 5.45-mm PSM automatic holstered at his hip, bringing the barrel halfway up from the leather before a starburst twinkled at the figure's hip and two mule-kicks, each separated by a microsecond, punched him squarely in the heart.

Cage saw the sound-suppressed HK MP5-KA4's 9-mm hollowpoint rounds score textbook shot patterns, exploding inside the terrorist's chest cavity and shredding his heart, lungs, and sections of his ribcage.

Other Leisure Books by Kyle Maning:

SWASTIKA
KILLPOINT
MIA

· KYLE MANING ·

BLOOD STORM

LEISURE BOOKS NEW YORK CITY

Although this is a work of fiction, the portrayals of the Proteus Chain and the assault on 'Uqba bin Nafi are based on fact. The author wishes to thank Colonel C. William Bascomb, U.S. Special Forces, retired, and Lieutenant Colonel Arye Eytan of the Israeli Defense Forces for their invaluable assistance in the writing of this book.

A LEISURE BOOK®

June 1990

Published by

Dorchester Publishing Co., Inc.
276 Fifth Avenue
New York, NY 10001

Printed in the United States of America.

When a man hath no freedom to fight for at home,
  Let him combat for that of his neighbors;
Let him think of the glories of Greece and of Rome,
  And get knocked on his head for his labors.

To do good to mankind is the chivalrous plan,
  And is always as nobly requited;
Then battle for freedom wherever you can,
  And if not shot or hanged, you'll get knighted.

—Lord Byron

There are two laws discrete,
Not reconciled,
Law for man, and law for things;
The last builds town and fleet,
But it runs wild,
And doth the man unking.

—Ralph Waldo Emerson

Prologue: ONE

In the Gen III monocular Night Observation Device that fit securely over Logan Cage's right eye, the blacked-out terrorist hardsite in the desert wasteland 200 feet below him showed up clearly against a solid green field.

Its layout was exactly as the high-resolution photos from an orbiting KH-11 "Big Bird" reconsat had shown: three barracks-style longhouses surrounding a dirt compound with a tin-roofed vehicle shed at its center.

Cage checked the luminous dial of his Huer chronometer.

The time was 3:47 A.M.

Those inside the terrorist camp would be in maggot dreamland. Z-Comm's top merc allowed himself the luxury of a grim smile.

Their rest was just beginning. Z-Comm was about to put them to sleep forever.

As the Reaper's emissaries, Cage and company would sprinkle them with full-auto stardust.

Rockabye and good night.

Against the indigo blackness of a moonless sky, the black parachutes on which the shadow warriors drifted earthward from the high-altitude dropzone would be virtually invisible to observers on the ground.

In the combat blacksuits they wore and black Balaclava battle masks that surrounded their heads, they would be as unseeable as avenging specters dropping out of hell to visit bloody destruction on their earthly targets.

"Thirty seconds to dustoff," Cage spoke into the rice-grain mike positioned in front of his mouth on a curved steel wire. "Sing out . . . Zabriskie?"

"Yo."

"Proffit?"

"Yo."

"Domino?"

"Yo."

"MacBeth?"

"Yo."

A beat, and Cage spoke again into the mike.

"Okay. Fifteen seconds. Put some thunder up your butts and hit the ground running."

Down below, even as they slept unsuspectingly, the terrorist splinter group calling itself the Apocalypse Battalion was already cold meat on a slab.

The unlucky ones would be those scum specimens who survived to be taken prisoners.

Z-Comm's mission plan called for sparing the lives of two of the targets for heliborne extraction, followed by interrogation at the trilateral U.S.-Israeli-Chadian command post across the border in Ouadi Doum, Chad.

The survivors would be handed over to the spooks and the mad doctors with the long hypodermic needles.

They would spill their guts and die slow, horrible deaths as the intelligence ghouls sucked their souls and brains out of their bodies and threw the empty human husks into the burn bag when they were finished.

A hard judgement call? Yeah, for sure. But Z-Comm had no problems with acting as death's covert messengers.

Tonight's target had long since crossed the blood-red line which divided those who merited the rights of due process from those who could be exterminated with no more remorse than fumigating a nest of plague-carrying rodents.

Those below had chosen to cast their lot with the army of mindless destruction in the crossfire hurricane that raged across international boundaries, leaving death on a global scale in its grisly wake.

The self-styled revolutionaries had forged a blood pact with the devil, and would now pay their death dues to the emergency surgeons who plunged from the sky bearing the steel-squirting implements of sterilizing fire.

Destruction would be swift, sure.

And silent as the grave.

There wouldn't be a line in the papers or a "sound bite" in the media to call attention to what went down.

Death would arrive in the predawn blackness and depart without leaving behind a trace of its grim presence.

The terrorists had waged their battle in the center ring of a media circus that spotlighted their twisted agendas.

It had taken a long time for society to come to its senses and realize that it was playing into the terrorists' hands by dancing to their tune.

Retaliation would now be meted out in clandestine doses.

It was time to play the only game Terrorist International understood.

Hardball.

Shadow warriors would deal brutal punishment in the dark of night. Spectral death specialists would bring the terrorists' own tactics home to them with surgical precision.

The new name of the game would be SLAM —Search, Locate, and Annihilate Missions.

The exterminators would be as impossible to trace as the soul-less killers who preyed on society had been. They would leave no track, no record of their bloody deeds.

Nothing in print, on videotape, or in the minds of men.

The war would go underground. The unending tempo of kill and counterkill would recede from the headlines, entering a new phase where it would be slugged out in the murky darkness of clandestine operations, a limbo hellzone where blood rules were the only rules, where survival was the only word that was worth a fucking damn.

A covert-action nightmare world.

Z-Comm's world.

"Get ready," Cage said, "to take out the garbage."

The strike team braced for action.

The ground rushed toward the shadow warriors with dizzying speed.

Prologue: TWO

Roarke shuffled from the darkened barracks into the still desert night. Although the air temperature had dropped from a daytime high of 120 degrees Fahrenheit to a cool 40 degrees, the sand still radiated heat. The terrorist felt the warmth on his face when the wind stilled enough to let it cut through.

Dipping into the right breast pocket of his safari jacket, Roarke extracted a crumpled cigaret pack containing Jordanian Farid plain-ends that had been liberally laced with Lebanese hashish, stuck one between his lips, and lit the twisted end.

Roarke had begun mixing his hash with cheap tobacco, Arab-fashion, after hearing that it improved sexual performance in men.

The terrorist dragged sleepily, sucking the

narcotic smoke deep into his lungs. It was against camp regs to smoke in the open, but Roarke didn't care. The doctored cigaret tasted like goat dung, but Roarke didn't complain. He didn't smoke them for the taste.

For the past year he had been troubled by a recurring nightmare from which he'd awaken in cold sweats. The dream was always the same. In it, demonic specters with flame-belching eyes and mouths chased Roarke through a jellylike medium. The harder he ran, the slower he moved. When they finally caught him, Roarke was torn to shreds by the hellish apparitions.

The only thing that steadied Roarke's nerves was stretching his legs in the cool night air and toking a few hash-laced Farids. The American spy satellites that might register the flicker of flame from eight miles above the earth be damned.

Roarke needed what he needed.

And what Roarke needed, he had always managed to take, one way or the other.

Running his fingers through his shock of close-cropped blond hair, the terrorist turned his face toward the sky. It was a moonless night and stars peppered the inverted black bowl of the heavens.

Taking another drag, Roarke turned his head, trying to name the constellations. That's when he saw something that made him freeze in panic.

The panic came from his subconscious mind, which flashed a danger signal before

Roarke's senses had time to orient him. At first, the stars seemed to disappear from a patch low on the western horizon, only to twinkle back into view a heartbeat later.

Roarke's next thought was that the hash was making him hallucinate some big bird flying across his visual field, although he realized that this was absurd even as the thought flashed across his consciousness.

It took two full seconds before the terrifying truth dawned on Roarke.

The figures were manshapes.

Paratroops dropping into the compound.

Roarke watched in horrified fascination.

It was almost like in his dream, he thought in stupefied panic.

The first spectral shape was already down, the chute blowing away like a black shadow rolling across the dusty desertscape. Behind the point man, another figure hit the ground, rolled, and got to its feet, cutting the black chute loose from its harness.

Already, it was too late for Roarke. The terrorist saw the first figure swerve, come up clutching a weapon in target acquisition.

The Sandman was about to put him to sleep the hard way.

Frantically, he scrabbled for the Soviet 5.45-mm PSM automatic holstered at his hip, bringing the barrel halfway up from the leather before a starburst twinkled at the ghostshape's hip and two mule-kicks, each separated by a microsecond, punched him squarely in the heart.

Cage saw the sound-suppressed HK MP5-KA4's 9-mm hollowpoint rounds score textbook shot patterns, exploding inside the terrorist's chest cavity and shredding his heart, lungs, and sections of his ribcage.

The gaping entry wound in the badguy's upper torso was grim testament to the Teflon-encased Glaser Safety slugs' effectiveness at close range, as well as the "tap-tap"—two shots to the head or chest—method of quick garbage-disposal preferred for SMG killing operations.

Bloody gobbits of razored flesh sprayed from the terrorist's back as Roarke spun on his heels, flung his arms in the air, and flopped onto his face in the yellow desert dust.

Damn.

The dying zap artist hadn't made much noise, but then again, terrorists weren't known to be heavy sleepers.

For Cage and his crew, the op was now compromised. Had to be. The element of surprise was gone. Without needing to be told, each covert warrior braced for the firefight they knew lay dead ahead.

Cage moved fast, signing to Zabriskie and Proffit to take the leftmost barracks while he and Domino moved on the one directly ahead.

MacBeth would do his one-merc-army number on the rightmost building. As Z-Comm's merc honcho and the deadly female commando hustled for the barracks, each folded back the Gen III scopes so that the light-amplification tubes were in a retracted position at the tops of their black-masked heads.

Although this meant that they'd have to rely on normal night vision to sight on their targets, it was a necessary precaution against the "bloom-out" that would occur if even a single light were switched on inside by a suddenly awakened terrorist.

The sudden presence of light would be amplified by the nightscope into a blinding starflash that would paralyze the wearer of the visual-amplification device.

Cage kicked in the door, nodded at Domino, and went inside in a sideways crouch, the MP5-KA4 jerking to and fro. Domino followed close behind, her sound-suppressed MAC 10 poised for action. Almost simultaneously, the lights came on.

Two wild-eyed men were pointing AKM rifles their way. The *Avtomat Kalashnikova Modernizirovanii* assault weapons were more compact than the Soviet standard issue AKs, but every bit as deadly. One man shouted in what sounded like German and cut loose with a burst of 7.62-mm lead that sent wood chips flying and slug fragments ricocheting everywhere as the heavy-caliber hitters slammed home.

The Z-Comm deathbringers opened up with their own lethal heat. The SIONIC-silenced SMG in Cage's fist coughed.

Whispering death claimed the violencer on

the far right as his head belched a tomato-sized ball of bloody brain tissue.

Domino's dance partner was so preoccupied with trying to hit the fast-dodging female merc with his AKM bursts that he didn't even notice his pard getting splattered all over the walls by Cage's SMG quickburst.

Leaning on the trigger, he unloaded most of his 30-round AKM clip at the deadly, black-clad Valkyrie before a figure-eight of .45-caliber rounds from the MAC in Domino's hands stitched him open from throat to belt-line and sent the night's third kill sprawling across the floor in a black pool of his own rivering blood.

While Cage and Domino hustled through the maggot nest searching for new threats, the rest of Z-Comm was kicking ass in its own right.

Clutching a SPAS-16 bullpup in his big fists, Bear MacBeth pivoted as a hail of SovBloc autofire whipped the sand at his booted feet into miniature volcanos.

Tracking on the trajectory of the 7.62s, the Bear saw the manshape hunched atop the barracks roof. Fire erupted from the AKM's barrel as the terrorist unleashed a commie-caliber hellstorm at the black-garbed invader.

Rolling out of the death stream, MacBeth came up crouch-firing a whirlwind of double-zero shot in savage answer. The roofgunner toppled, rolled down, and hit the ground in a pulverized heap.

Bear made tracks for the barracks door, but changed course just as it flew open and twin geysers of chattering death belched in ugly unison from either side, while a third line of fire chattered from the shattered window right beside it.

The big merc's course correction saved his ass in the nick of time, as he booked for cover behind a water pump a little to his left and returned fire in a quick follow-through.

A pulsebeat earlier, Proffit and Zabriskie had pitched stun grenades into the third barracks building. Of the five death soloists inside, two had tried their luck and wound up leaking all over the floor, while the other two had put down their weapons.

Nice and easy.

Proffit and Zabriskie hooked up with the Bear just as MacBeth was getting tired of playing human target and was preparing to move on the building.

Zabriskie had a better idea. He threaded a 40-mm Mecar CN gas shell into his M16A2 assault weapon. The Mecar shells needed no special ammo or muzzle adapters. They could be launched using virtually any conventional rifle round. The irritant canister would flush the human rats from their desert nest.

Zabriskie aimed at the window and a trigger-pull sent the irritant can tumbling through into the dark interior. A few moments later, coughing men staggered out the open door through clouds of noxious brown fumes.

Three terrorists had been flushed from the barracks and each was feeling lucky. AKM fire rotored from their hips as they dodged for cover. A hail of full-auto death gave the terrorists permanent relief from the itchy eyes and runny noses of CN gas.

Cage and Domino came out after a quick room-by-room of the first barracks revealed that, apart from the terrorists already encountered, it was empty.

Z-Command linked up. Zabriskie used the team's compact AN/PRC 112 combat radio to call in the extraction chopper.

The Huey Blackhawk was already in the air, awaiting the strike team's call-in.

The slick driver, equipped with Gen III nightseeing goggles for invisible navigation, would home in on the transponder signal that the versatile AN/PRC 112 also transmitted. Less than three minutes later, the helo's rotors beat out a steady thuk-a-thuk as the rotorcraft flew a hedge-hopping course to dodge hostile radar.

Z-Comm hustled its two stunned captives into the slick's passenger/cargo bay. There was only one thing left to be done. Cross the *t*'s and dot the *i*'s.

Fitting a 40-mm rifle grenade into his M16A2, Zabriskie launched the HEAT round at one of the buildings. Thunder convulsed the desert night as a broiling toadstool of devouring flame reared obscenely from the barracks roof.

Twice more, Zabriskie repeated the ritual of deadly purification, obliterating all traces of the terrorist cancer forever.

The slick lifted off into the moonless night, the explosions below buffeting the steel-hulled dragonfly as it swung sharply to the south, toward the secret base across the Libyan border, in Ouadi Doum, Chad.

All systems were go.

Prologue: THREE

While Z-Comm was being debriefed, the soul-suckers were preparing to go to work on the night delivery of fresh human meat.

The mad doctors were the modern equivalent of the torturers of the Spanish Inquisition. Only, instead of the rack and thumbscrews, they used mind altering drugs and psychological conditioning.

The end result, however, was little different from that produced by the dungeons of the fifteenth century.

From here on in, the spooks took over the show.

Z-Comm had taken care of the grunt work. Now it was the turn of the so-called intelligence professionals to get their crack at the clandestine operation.

That was okay with Cage and company.

As far as Z-Comm went, the bad guys had brought retribution down on their own heads. Of course, the mercs had about as much use for the spooks and their kind as a mongoose has for a spitting cobra.

But sometimes the compromises and trade-offs of the invisible war they had signed on to fight made it necessary to hold hands with the clammy Caspers for awhile.

This was one such occasion. From the moment the op had gone green, the interrogation crew was set up in Chad for the live prisoners the mission had called for.

A high body count might have been the mission's primary objection, sure, but the intelligence bonanza reaped from breaking one of the captured hardguys would be worth its weight in hijacked 747s.

Who knew what they'd be able to tell once they got shot full of the gonzo juice that the Sister Morphines had in their long, sharp needles?

In any case, the clandestine sponsors in Congress and the CIA who had pushed for the Libyan SLAM raid wanted to get their money's worth, and the spooks who'd orchestrated it were men who aimed to please their paymasters.

The two captured terrorists were a man and a woman. The two had been in bed together at the time of the raid. They had been held in the same state of nakedness in which they'd been captured in a chicken-wire cage for a couple of hours. The spooks and the Chadian military brass had done a paper-shuffling act while actually watching them through two-way mirrors.

Both had been given a chance to willingly cooperate.

Neither would.

That was okay with the spooks.

The male terrorist was dragged kicking and screaming from the holding tank and brought into the interrogation room. The spooks made a point of roughing the guy up in front of his girlfriend. The dope docs said it would soften him up.

The interrogation room was sterile. Very little was in it, but then again it wasn't supposed to be the Presidential Suite at the Helmsley Palace. A padded clinical bed stood at its center, directly beneath a high-intensity light that shone down from the ceiling on a long metal track.

Mounted on a tripod a few feet from the bed was an industrial video camera. Black cables snaked from the camera to a table on which sat a VCR unit and a multitrack tape deck. A CIA technician punched a few buttons on the sound rig and stood up to crouch behind the camera as the terrorist was dragged in by two Chadian regulars in camo fatigues.

As they strapped the naked terrorist into the clinical bed with his arms lashed tightly against his sides, the tech focused the camera on him, checking the visual output against a TV monitor screen. When he was satisfied it was properly set up, the spook Spielberg returned to the tableful of recording equipment.

When the naked, terrified prisoner was securely strapped in, the two soul-suckers made their grand entrance.

The brain-drainers were flanked by a contingent of CIA and Israeli Mossad spooks and Chadian military personnel in camo fatigues.

As a means of solving a jurisdictional dispute that had arisen during the planning stages of the op, the interrogators represented intelligence organizations of all three participating nations. Spy scandals notwithstanding, there was nothing out of the ordinary in a joint intelligence venture of this kind.

While the assholes in the news media might raise high holy hell over allies spying on each other, the spooks knew that the lion's share of espionage was, in point of fact, directed at friends more often than enemies.

And with good reason too.

For one thing, even allies didn't have mutually coinciding interests all the time. For another, it was a hell of a lot easier to spy on a friendly power than on an enemy.

Intelligence was a valuable commodity. U.S. intel on Arab troop movements could be exchanged for Soviet tanks captured by Israel. Espionage was a dirty hustle. The players bought cheap and sold dear. Intelligence was the street. No more, no less.

Sometimes, though, events forced normally intelligence-greedy countries to pool their efforts toward a common cause. In this case, the murder of an American foreign-services attaché in Brussels a few weeks before the SLAM raid had sent ripples throughout the U.S. intelligence community.

The radical terror crew calling itself the Apocalypse Battalion that claimed responsibility for the hit had carried out similar strikes against CIA targets abroad, although few reports had made it into the noncovert media.

This time the "freedom-fighters" had pushed their luck.

The retaliatory strike was given the go-order, but certain logistical problems still remained. One of these was covert air support.

Like many terror units that had become household words—the PLO, the Provisional IRA, and Hizballah, to name a few—the Apocalypse Battalion's training camp was located inside Libya, and the only pro-Western power in the region that might allow its territory to be used as an airbase was Chad.

The black Chadians hated the Arab Libyans' guts. It was a long-running feud. The Chadians claimed that the Libyans had sold them into slavery hundreds of years ago.

The fact that the United States happened to have been the major purchaser of those very same black slaves was a fact that had never been forgotten. Little Chad accepted money and arms from its big Uncle Sam, but had never totally trusted Whitey.

The Israelis, on the other hand, while technically the "Zionist enemy" to the tiny North African Moslem nation, had in fact a long history of cooperation with African states. Operation Thunderball, the lightning raid on Entebbe, had used Chad as a staging area for Israeli aircraft.

Chad had served a similar purpose for the present raid deep into Qaddafi's homeland to cancel the Apocalypse Battalion's license to kill.

The first soul-sucker introduced himself to the terrorist as "Mr. Paul." In reality, his name was Howard Johnson. Like in the hotel chain. Johnson had learned his grim tradecraft in Vietnam.

There also, he had developed an insensitivity to human suffering born, in large part, by seeing what the Viet Cong had done to a Vietnamese woman whom he had loved. When they had finished with her, she had been turned into a submental idiot without a tongue or a vagina. When the CIA spooks had recruited Johnson for his medical expertise in interrogating VC prisoners, he had been quick to accept.

The Israeli doctor, who introduced himself to the naked prisoner as "Mr. Molok," was of the same mindset. At the age of twelve he had begun a five-year stay in the Nazi concentration camps of World War II. At Auschwitz, he had become an assistant to Dr. Mengele, and there had been transformed into a Jewish version of the Nazi killer.

Both "Paul" and "Molok" were twisted psychopaths, perverted sadists who had the capacity to subject their victims to cold, clinical, calculated mind-destruction. Unfortunately, they were also as necessary to modern intelligence as spy satellites and armies of clandestine mercenaries.

At a nod from one of the spooks, Mr. Paul tied a length of rubber tubing around the naked subject's right arm. Mr. Molok inspected an IV bag and trundled it close to the bed. He handed the long, needle-tipped tube to Mr. Paul.

The American smiled and plunged the hypodermic tip into the bulging artery on the naked man's forearm. His cold gray eyes were alive with some unreadable emotion.

"I'm going to take you higher than a junkie in a space shuttle," he began softly as the terrorist's eyes glazed over and his body went into convulsions. *"I'm going to break every bone in your mind."*

Z-Comm put the wraps on the debriefing session.

It had taken a little over an hour.

They had gone over the mission's events from chute-down to shoot-down.

Their reports would be entered into classified intelligence dossiers bearing color-coded warning covers marked EXDIS, for exclusive dissemination to a tightly restricted group of insiders as well as to intelligence supercomputers on three continents.

Cage headed for the coffee machine on a table against a wall. This would make it his fifth cup of the night, but what the hell, a little more caffeine wouldn't kill him, and anyway, what if it did?

"Have some of this, my friend."

Cage turned. The Israeli colonel held out a half pint of American bourbon. Colonel Zvi Harvassi of the elite commando group, Sayaret Motkal, was the Israeli contribution to the military-intelligence team that had planned the SLAM raid on the terror camp.

The terms of the joint mission were that the op would be a team effort in all but one vital respect: Because the terrorists had targeted Americans only, it would be U.S. citizens who acted as their executioners.

The colonel, therefore, could only serve in a support capacity, assisting with the logistical planning and sitting in on the debriefing session as an observer.

The American merc nodded and the colonel poured the booze into his paper cup, then poured the rest of the bottle into the cup in his own hand. Both men downed the whiskey, feeling it spread its warmth through their veins.

"L'Chaim," said the colonel.

"To crime," Cage answered.

"A shame I wasn't able to play a more active role in the mission, Colonel Cage," Haravassi said. "It's the kind of op my men have perfected."

"We did okay," Cage said, the faintest edge in his voice.

"Yes, of course," Harvassi told him. "A pity also that the soulless zombies in the next room must now have their way with the prisoners."

"I know what you mean," Cage returned, looking the military man straight in the eyes.

To men who had been tested in the crucible of battle, it was a violation of a universal, though unspoken, code to throw the enemy to the dogs.

Like Harvassi, Cage had been blooded in battle in a war where the rules of combat applied to the vanquished and the victorious alike. At least as far as the sides they'd fought on were concerned.

But that had been years ago.

This was a dirtier, bloodier, far more dangerous war he was now a soldier in.

It was a clandestine war and it was played by rules that could never be applied in the light of day. A soldier in such a war had to abide by those rules or leave the firezone to others prepared to accept them.

A bloodcurdling scream suddenly echoed through the debriefing room.

For a moment, both Harvassi and Cage turned and stared hard at the debriefing room's olive drab walls.

A terrorist was just beginning to realize where he was.

Hell.

BOOK ONE:

Odds Are You Won't Live to See Tomorrow

ONE

Y*es, he was sure of it!*

The man was Hans Kleist, the Nazi they had called the Ghoul of Treblinka. Even after more than 40 years, the Ghoul's white, corpselike face was still instantly recognizable.

It was, after all, a face he had seen in countless nightmares; a face that had tormented him for almost half a century. The black pushbutton eyes, the high forehead, patrician nose, and oversized ears. The skin with its cadaverous whiteness, unlined and blank as the plastic skin of a doll.

Yes, there was no doubt about it.

It was the Ghoul.

And he was only feet from where Leonard Harris sat. Born Hrabchak, Harris had been only 12 years old when he had been dragged by stormtroopers from his village of Kielce in southern Poland and herded into a railroad car to begin a long, harrowing journey with the Treblinka Concentration Camp as its final destination.

Hundreds in his one car alone died along the way. Harris remembered all too vividly how those who became too weak to stand were left to lie where they fell, trampled beneath the feet of the imprisoned human cattle aboard the boxcar.

One of those who perished en route was Harris's Uncle Ivor. Harris still vividly remembered how he had fought to keep his place by a chink in the wooden slats that made up the wall of the boxcar where fresh air trickled through.

Unable to leave his precious spot, he'd called for his uncle, but the old man hadn't answered. Harris had known that he was already lying among the corpses littering the floor of the car.

But the horror was yet to begin when the train carrying those whom the Nazi Reich deemed unworthy of life had reached its final destination. There, those who'd survived the week-long rail journey first learned the true meaning of hell.

It was also at that point that Harris caught his first glimpse of Hans Kleist, the Ghoul of Treblinka.

Schmeisser-armed SS troops forced the stumbling survivors from the line of cattle cars to form a long line which shuffled through the barbed-wire gates of the concentration camp.

There, an SS officer in a field-gray overcoat and peaked cap bearing the elite death's head insignia of the *Schutzstaffel* selected the inmates who would be taken immediately to the gas chambers and those who would survive a while longer, as slave labor for the Nazi master race.

Because Harris was big for his age and strong, he was sent—with a flick of the SS officer's finger—onto the line for those who would live. Harris was to see that effeminate finger flick over and over in the course of the months he toiled at the extermination center.

It had become burned into his brain, the symbol of everything corrupt and evil in the world. That fey, effortless crook of the finger that had sent some directly to the crematoria, others to labor like plough animals before death claimed them. It expended less energy than it took to kill a bug.

It seemed to say that to Kleist a human life wasn't even worth more than the minimal effort required to flick a finger.

Now, almost a half century after that day of horror, Leonard Harris had recognized that same flick of the finger in a café on the Leidseplein in Amsterdam, Holland, as he idly watched a man signal a waiter to bring the check over the remains of his *koffietafel.*

At first it hadn't registered, and Harris had

moved on to admire the figure of a young girl playing a Chopin nocturne on the violin to a ghetto-blaster providing taped accompaniment. Then the memory moved into synch with reality and Harris froze with shock.

A cold sweat broke out on the back of his neck. He turned again. His eyes stared at the maggoty white corpse-flesh of the Ghoul's face, and Harris was catapulted into an acid flashback of nightmarish intensity.

Harris had been an American citizen for over 40 years. He had anglicized his name to make it sound more American. The tattoo on his upper arm that had borne the numbers the Third Reich had given him in place of his identity had been painfully removed by surgery.

He had not spoken his native Polish since being liberated by British soldiers in 1945. He had tried to surgically remove a past he despised by becoming as American as possible, assimilating himself as completely as he could into the culture of his adopted homeland. Harris had married an American girl and settled down in Stockton, California, his idea of an all-American city.

And now, in the space of an eye blink, four decades of life as a U.S. citizen fell away, exposing the 12-year-old Polish boy who had fallen through the cracks into the molten center of hell. Harris trembled violently. Memories he had long supressed flooded back in a tidal wave that made his brain reel.

The cosmic irony was that it was Harris's

first trip abroad since coming to the United States. He had become assimilated into American society to the extent that his job had been crucially linked to his country's military defense.

After the war he had gone to college, majoring in electrical engineering. The company he started manufactured sophisticated defense electronics. Harris had come to Holland to strike an important deal with a European subcontractor. Too important to delegate, it was a deal he had to cut himself.

Anger rose in Leonard Harris's chest as he watched the Nazi sip champagne and talk with a young woman and another man seated with them at the table. This second man was not familiar, but Harris recognized the type he represented all too well.

The shaven head riding a bull neck, the long puckered scar running down the right side of his face, the powerfully muscled shoulders, and the quiet menace he exuded like a hellish stench marked him as one of the Nazis who had carried out bloody killing on the orders of men like Kleist.

Then Harris realized that the party at the other table had noticed him staring at them. A cold fear took hold of Harris as Kleist, the bald giant, and the blonde woman turned to stare back at him.

Harris felt as though they could read his mind. He felt as if they had x-ray vision that could penetrate through his flesh and see the pumping heart and the churning organs.

Harris hastily pulled Dutch banknotes from his pockets and dropped them on the table in a rumbled heap. Staggering to his feet, he left the cafe as quickly as possible.

Out on the cobbled pavement of the Leidseplein, Harris turned. He saw the trio get up and leave, heading straight toward him. Although Harris was scared out of his wits, he forced himself to remain calm. After all, he thought, they might not have noticed him after all. How could they know who he was? He was letting his imagination run away with him.

A taxi came by on the Marnixstraat and Harris hailed it, feeling instantly relieved as the small cab sped along the broad boulevard. Risking a look through the rear windshield, Harris saw the trio crossing the Leidseplein behind him. Had they really been able to identify him as a former Treblinka inmate, he said to himself, they would have certainly made an attempt to follow him. But they had not.

Harris felt completely secure by the time he reached his hotel. He went to his room and contemplated what action to take next.

The only thing to do, he decided, would be to phone the American Embassy in Amsterdam and tell them about the Ghoul. The Embassy people would investigate the matter. It would then be out of his hands.

Harris picked up the phone and asked the operator for an outside line. The American-accented female voice that answered the Embassy's phone further reassured Harris. Harris told the woman what he had seen and she put him on to an Embassy staffer who took his statement.

The staffer told Harris not to worry. If the Nazi was on the international list of wanted war criminals, then efforts would be made to apprehend him. The staffer thanked Harris for his help and wished him a pleasant stay in Amsterdam.

Hanging up the phone, Harris felt much better. What he needed now was some bourbon. He had cultivated a taste for the Kentucky sour mash until it was the only whiskey he felt comfortable drinking. Like everywhere else in Europe, they served lousy bourbon in Holland, Harris had discovered, but right now a double bourbon on the rocks at the hotel bar sounded mighty good.

Harris went down to the bar in the lobby and had a couple of drinks. By his third double bourbon he had almost, but not quite, forgotten about the Ghoul of Treblinka. He also began thinking about something he had been meaning to try when in Holland but hadn't had a chance to yet, something besides seeing the windmills and the blooming tulips.

The government-subsidized red-light district had been recommended to him by a friend who had been to Amsterdam the year before. Harris had the address of a house that catered to diversions of a kinkier nature than most. He had often visited such bitch goddesses in the States, but had heard some interesting stories about the range and variety of services available in this part of the world.

Harris left the hotel and stood outside waiting for a cab. He did not notice the Volvo sedan that made a rapid U-turn and pulled to a screaming halt in front of him. Nor did he notice the stocky, bald man that had been sitting beside the Nazi earlier that afternoon come up behind him and shove him into the back seat of the car, then quickly get in after him and shut the door.

"What the hell is this?" Harris cried out.

"This, Jew," the blonde woman said from the front seat, "is your personal final solution."

With a grunt that might have been a laugh, the big man raised a silenced automatic pistol and fired once into Harris's face. Rounding a corner, the car pulled down an alley, and the bald man kicked Harris's corpse into a pile of garbage.

The Volvo sped off into the street and was ditched a few minutes later, many miles from where it had been stolen.

TWO

Sam Proffit felt uncomfortable, three ways.

For one thing, Proffit didn't like crowds and he was now the center of attention.

For another, he didn't like wearing anything fancier than a ratty pair of Levis and a slogan T-shirt. He was now all duded up in some expensive Italian threads his girlfriend Penny had bought him and forced him to wear. He felt like a fucking fruit.

Worse than a fucking fruit. He felt like Harry Zabriskie.

And even though some art critics had called him the most promising American sculptor in 20 years, Proffit usually felt awkward around his own art. For him, the turn-on was in the act of creation itself. What happened afterward didn't matter. Not to him at least.

To the arty set it was a different story. The exhibition of Sam Proffit's work represented the combined output of the last five years. The exhibition hall at the Portland Museum of Fine Art was packed with people.

It was already being hailed as a milestone for the young artist—young, at least, by the standards of the art world which called anybody under 40 "young"—and had established Proffit internationally.

Nevertheless, Proffit felt as out of place as the guy in the beer commercial whose idea of a masterpiece was a cold brew with a nice sudsy head on it.

He felt like telling every chickenshit well-wisher who shook his hand and told him what a fucking genius he was to take a flying fuck at a rolling doughnut hole. And if not for Penny, Proffit might have done just that. But she was keeping a tight rein on him, making sure that she was close at hand to steer well-wishers away when her man's temper was on the verge of overload.

So far it had worked. Clutching a cocktail glass in his hand, Proffit was buttonholed by a matronly woman holding a small poodle. The poodle was dyed hot pink. The woman was an influential art critic. She gushed effusively over Proffit's work.

What Proffit didn't notice were the men who had just entered the gallery. In their mid-thirties, the men had a different walk then the rest of the chic people.

They stood out in the crowd like purple gorillas in a nudist colony.

Had Proffit noticed, he would have seen the telltale bulges of automatic weapons beneath their windbreakers.

The Champs Elysees had been swept by a drenching rain that morning. Now the Arc de Triomphe hunkered against a cloudless sky and the trees lining the park below Le Rond Point on either side were reflected on the still-wet surface of the broad boulevard that stretched from the River Seine to the Place de la Concorde.

Domino had come out with the rest of the Parisians to enjoy the spring weather. The sun was now shining brightly, but patches of dampness had not yet dried on the walls of the ancient buildings surrounding her. People bustled all around, but she felt distant and detached.

After the raid inside Libya, she had needed a place to go to work out the kinks. In Paris she could get away from herself. Be totally alone.

You could be alone in New York or Berlin or Venice or Los Angeles, but only in Paris could you find that special solitude that allowed you to look at your inmost thoughts, clearly and undistorted.

She had rented a room in a small pension in the fifth arrondissement off the Boulevard St. Michael and kept to herself. The weather had been rainy. Domino had sat in cafes, sipping cafe au lait and reading paperback novels. She even wrote poetry.

She had been wrestling with a problem since the raid. The look on the terrorist's face when his stomach had been blown away by a round of .45 ACP lead from her MAC was still with her.

This had never happened before.

She had always been able to bounce right back after an op, no matter how extended the time-frame or how punishing the action. Now, for the first time, Domimo was tormented by memories of the bloody task she had performed. The memories would come in sleep, wrenching her violently awake in a feverish sweat.

Domino wasn't sure she could continue with the mercenary life any longer. She had heard about others who had reached such an impasse.

You arrived at a point where you couldn't go on anymore. You lost your nerve. That loss could—and due to the nature of the savage endgame in which she was a player, almost certainly *would*—result in her death.

She did not want to die. Not yet. She wasn't ready yet. This was another frightening realization. Domino had long since given up caring about whether she lived or died. One way or the other, it didn't make a hell of a lot of difference.

She had told no one about these recent feelings. It was her special secret, her personal cross.

Once she had cared. Years before, married to a cop in Miami. Then, she had been a mother and a wife. Her husband had been a good man, and her daughter a beautiful child of six.

One day the savages came.

The savages came and took her man and her child.

Murdered them.

And went free.

Her husband had died twice. Once, in Nam, where they had cut out his soul and left a burned-out husk behind. He had died a second death in the mean streets of South Miami. At the hands of the savages.

Domino had gone after the cocaine cowboys who'd snuffed her man and child. She had become the snow honcho's mistress. He had never suspected a thing. He had fallen in love with the Grim Reaper, given his heart to a vengeance-driven female who was as deadly as she was beautiful.

On the day Domino killed the abominable snowman, the *coquero* and his snow queen were alone together on his yacht. There were sharks in the blue Gulf waters off Cedar Key. She threw him in, and when he thrashed around, pulled out an automatic pistol and began shooting the sharks.

Driven mad with the taste of blood, the savage creatures went into a feeding frenzy. The Cuban drug baron pleaded for his life. It didn't do him a lick of good. Domino watched as he was torn to bloody flayings by the frenzied carnivores of the deep.

She had mined the snow king's estate with C-4 charges. She set them off from a distance, blowing it all to hell and gone. Then she left. Just turned and walked away. She had thought it would end there; she had believed that the bloodletting would purge the shrieking demons infesting her soul.

But it hadn't.

And it couldn't.

Domino realized that she could never go back home again. Home was gone forever. She sold her belongings and contacted the man her husband had told her about.

The man from Special Operations in Nam.

Cage had never asked Domino why she wanted to take her chances in the bloodiest of macho death sports. She had never volunteered the answer either. To Cage, the woman warrior was a cold, ruthless, and efficient killing machine. But he had never been able to probe beyond the nail-hard surface. She was armored, that lady. Heavily armored.

Now, years later, Domino felt the first chink in that armor. Yet she had been in Paris for three weeks now and was no closer to deciding whether to stay in the game or walk away from it. She had taken a lover on her second day, a kid she had let pick her up in the Bois de Boulogne, more out of boredom than for any other reason. She had sent the gigolo packing the next morning. Sex was not the answer. What the hell was?

Suddenly, Domino felt a presence behind her. She turned. Harry Zabriskie stood with a lopsided grin on his handsome face. Domino wasn't even startled. It was just like Zabriskie to turn up in the most unlikely places.

"Go away, Harry," she said. "This is a private table."

Zabriskie sat down opposite her and waved the waiter over. "So you want to be ah-*lone*?" he said, mimicking Garbo's mannish voice. "Believe me, babe, with the vibes you've been throwing off, that ain't hard."

"How long were you standing there?" Domino asked.

"A couple of minutes," Zabriskie returned. "I'm in town for the International Defense Exhibition at the C.I.P. Convention Center. A friend of mine's got a booth there. Electronic equipment." The waitor, a bald guy in a short white jacket, came over. Zabriskie rattled off some high school French at the guy. The waiter's face colored.

"I think you just ordered a condom sauteed in poodle piss," Domino said. She ordered two Pernods in fluent French. The waiter went away, and returned a few minutes later with the drinks.

Neither Domino nor Harry saw the blue Citroen parked across the boulevard, the two trenchcoated figures inside vague blurs behind the rain-streaked windows.

Both men, however, had seen Zabriskie and Domino.

They watched both very carefully, clutching the automatic pistols at their sides as tightly as if they were the most precious possessions on earth.

Two thousand miles and three time zones away, it was eleven P.M. in Rio Di Janeiro. The city on the Brazilian coast had cooled from the heat of the day, but the air still felt like a Swedish sauna.

The tropical night was alive with sound and color. It was the second night of the Mardi Gras.

Logan Cage stood amid the throng watching the procession of bizarre floats and gaudily attired people pass like some strange hallucinatory episode he couldn't wake up from and didn't particularly want to.

Beside him, Frank McBeth paused from his beer drinking to admire the bevy of topless women who rode atop one of the floats. The float represented the sea god Poseidon. The women were costumed as mermaids. The bottom halves of their bodies tapered to large fins. They waved and blew kisses to the massive, boisterous crowd.

Hoisting his bottle of beer, MacBeth showed the women his approval.

"Fuckin' wayyyyyy to go! Shake those tits!"

MacBeth further showed his appreciation by shaking up the bottle of suds and, holding the bottle at groin level, squirting a jet of beer foam all over the place. Some of it struck a few of the locals nearby.

One man began cursing in loud Spanish while he wiped at his sopping face and the large beer stains on his loud, tropical print ensemble. Another, who carried a long spear and was dressed as a Samoan warrior, gestured menacingly at the Bear.

"Come on," Cage said, grabbing MacBeth. "I think I saw a bar back there." Turning, Cage saw the locals still shouting and shaking their fists. The guy with the spear was flipping them the bird. None of them followed, though. They were evidently smarter than they looked.

Cage permitted himself the luxury of a smile. He knew that bringing MacBeth along to Mardi Gras might present some problems, but the big guy was insistent on tagging along. He hadn't felt like coming back to the States yet for another go-round of construction work.

Neither Z-Commando noticed the group of men paralleling them as they elbowed through the thronged boulevard. Like most of the celebrants, the men were dressed in gaudy costumes.

They had their eyes on Cage and Bear every minute.

They were waiting for the right moment to buy them a couple of rounds.

Nine-millimeter.

THREE

The vz/64 Skorpion wasn't a very accurate weapon.

Or a very powerful one, for that matter.

The 9-mm Short (.380 Auto) cartridges it spat out at a 700-rpm cycling rate didn't have the stopping power of the tumbling manrippers a standard Uzi or an Ingram SMG fired.

Essentially, the Czech-manufactured gun was a glorified sidearm with full-auto capability, which therefore classed it as a machine pistol rather than a true submachine gun.

But the weapon's compact dimensions (the vz/64 used an "overhung" or "wraparound" bolt assembly) made it highly concealable, and it was a lethal contender in close-range, "killing-room" operations—two considerations that made it ideal for the death blitz to come.

Carlos the Jackal had taken advantage of the Skorpion's diminutive profile to make the autopistol world-renowned at the Munich massacre in 1978, giving the weapon its "PLO room-cleaner" nickname.

With a hollowpoint round chambered and another 19 identical twins in the Skorpion's 20-round box magazine, the Sad Sack clown with the red rubber nose who stood just a few yards from Cage and Bear had everything going for him, including the critical element of surprise.

Burst one would blow away the merc with the half-moon scar. Burst two would charcoal-broil the big guy with him. Because the vz/64 was inaccurate, there would certainly be casualties among the many bystanders.

No sweat, though. The terrorist had been thoroughly indoctrinated by North Korean instructors at the training camp in northern Iran. He was a soldier with a mission. There was nothing that could not be sacrificed for the cause he served.

Nothing and *nobody.*

And in case he failed to carry out his mission, there was backup all around. The shooter would be taken out if anything went wrong. The triggerman's pards would take care of any unforeseen surprises, or finish off the two kills if the job turned sloppy. They had the turkeys in a box.

Clownie would make damn certain that the strike went off without a hitch, though.

The hit had been ordered by Qaddafi himself. The Mad Dog of the Middle East had personally selected the hitman. It was a great privilege. He would not fail.

The terrorist torpedo watched the two targets enter the killzone. The space between two large parade floats gave him a clear line of fire, and the maze of streets behind him plenty of getaway room.

Now.

Now was the time to move.

Reaching under the colorful baggy clothes that made up his checkered clown suit, the bozo buttonman slid the Czech widowmaker from its custom rig and brought it into an upright position as he simultaneously thumbed off the safety and crouched into a two-handed target-shooting stance.

Sighting the weapon on the back of the big man's bald head, the Sad Sack shootist took a deep breath, held it, and squeezed the trigger.

His heart beat rapidly and time began to move in slow motion as he waited for the sight of flame jetting from the muzzle and the thunder of exploding bullets.

Thunder that never came.

A moment before the trigger reached the breakpoint, a semi-naked woman staggered drunkenly in front of him. She held out some brightly colored flowers, then gasped as she saw what was in clownie's white-gloved fists and flung the flowers into his face. The deadly bozo lost his balance and toppled sideways. The movement made his finger jerk reflexively on the trigger.

Rrrrriittttttttt!

Cage and MacBeth spun simultaneously, a heartbeat after hearing the telltale sound of automatic-weapons fire.

It was a sound they had heard all too often, and one which they reacted to instantly, violently, and without a second wasted. Combat senses shot lightning bolts along the pathways of their nerves. They were immediately alert and active.

At the same time as they scanned their visual fields for the source of the weapons report, the Z-Commandos were already in the process of whipping weapons of their own into quickfire position.

The first full-auto blaster out was Cage's Mini-Uzi SMG. The 9-mm manstopper had been nestled in a Velcro shoulder rig beneath Cage's lightweight sport jacket, awaiting just such a close encounter with the slime kind.

Cage didn't bother retracting the Mini-Uzi's wire buttstock. He only had time to thumb the select-fire stud from safety to full-auto. Besides, Cage had a strong enough grip to fire the Maggot Fumigator one-handed, and the compensating ports cut into the top of the Uzi's muzzle helped to stabilize the SMG.

Bear followed Cage a pulsebeat later, pulling the SPAS-16 bullpup pumpgun from the flex rig behind his back and chambering a 12-gauge cartridge.

The diminutive combat shotgun glittered in MacBeth's fists with cold, steel-blue menace. It was capable of hurricaning lethal heat with pinpoint accuracy. And MacBeth was a past master of the art, a virtuoso shotgunner.

Diagonally across the boulevard near one of the gaudy parade floats, a disturbance was taking place. The center of the disturbance was a clown.

A clown with a gun.

The shooter was now boxed in by the crowd surrounding him. But both Z-Commandos knew that this turn of events wouldn't last for very long. As long as the Skorpion stayed in the terrorist's hand, he had the equalizer.

There was an autoburst and two men who'd stepped in front of Bozo crumpled suddenly to the street. The crowd surrounding the cornered triggerman dispersed as he calmly ejected the spent 9-mm clip and snapped a fresh 20-round magazine into the vz/64's pistol grip.

With the bright red lips on the ghastly white face twisted into a perverse grimace of hate, the Bozo blaster hurled deadly fire at Cage and MacBeth.

The Z-Commandos returned the lethal heat. The shooter was blown apart by the combined firepower of the Uzi's 9-mm parabellum rounds and the steel whirlwind from Bear's SPAS-16 bullpup.

Then Bozo's backup kicked in.

Fire erupted from a float representing Captain Kidd and his merry band of pirates.

Only instead of rapiers, these lusty buccaneers wielded Kalashnikov AKs, blasting away with 7.62-mm gutbusters that tore up the pavement as Cage and Bear dove for cover behind another float. They were playing for keeps.

The procession of floats had come to a complete standstill. The boulevard was now as empty of people as it had been congested minutes before. The revelers cowered beneath parked cars and in the vestibules of adjoining buildings while the firefight raged on.

An Uziburst from Cage's blaster cut down one of the buccaneer shooters. He clutched his chest, toppling forward, and fell over the side of the float, hitting the blacktop with the sickening crack of splintering bones.

But there were still more of the puke pirate's lethal band left and the Z-Commandos were seriously outgunned. Their weapons couldn't deliver the range, accuracy, or raw blitzing firepower of the heavy-caliber AKs the opposition carried.

They needed to move, shake the opposition, get behind them and blow them away with surprise on their side. If they stayed pinned, they were dead meat. It was that simple. The 7.62 tumblers would buzzsaw through the flimsy protection offered by the float. A fragmenting slug could still contain enough kinetic energy to tear into their bodies and cut their innards to shreds.

Cage looked around. The street to either side was littered with empty bottles, testament to the fact that even the sanitation department had been partying for days.

Nearby, there was a car parked by the curbside. Cage told Bear to keep him covered and broke from cover. Hot steel sang at his heels as he dove behind the car and flipped open the gas-tank lid.

Cage used a straw he took from an empty soda can to siphon enough gas from the tank to fill two empty beer bottles. He tore his white cotton shirt and stuffed the rags into the mouths of the bottles.

"Now!" Cage hollered at MacBeth, who stood up from the barricade and, with a feral war whoop, cut loose with a 12-gauge whirlwind, drawing the badguys' fire away from Cage, who lit the rags on the Molotov cocktails and hurled them at the float.

Kuh-blammm! Kuh-BLAMMMMM!

A bloated mushroom ball of roaring flames rose from the street casting strobing flickers on the surrounding buildings. The Molotovs had landed short of the float, but the bullet-belching buccaneers were forced to take cover as the flames washed over them.

Everywhere, Mardi Gras parade floats were ablaze, the wind blowing the flames from one to the other as the Mardi Gras turned into a little corner of hell.

Cage and Bear hustled through the panicked crowds and darted down one of the narrow, alleylike backstreets. The alley fed out into another, broader street a few blocks away.

But they'd only succeeded in going from the frying pan to the fire.

Tires screeched. Another hit crew of terrorist shooters piled out of a compact car that had roared up the street toward Cage and Bear.

They had murder in their eyes and iron in their fists.

"I say we do it now."

"No. It will be too sloppy. There are too many bystanders around. And too many *flics* as well."

"To hell with the bastards, and the damned cops too."

The big man with the shaven head in the back seat of the Citroen on the Champs Elysees made the final decision.

"Follow them," he said in a voice full of rocks. "I will tell you when the operation is to proceed."

The rest of the men did as ordered. To do otherwise would be to number themselves among the dead.

FOUR

The International Defense Exhibition was being held at the C.I.P. Convention Center, a plate-glass-and-steel coliseum in central Paris. Manufacturers of weapons and military electronics from around the world had set up booths and displays of the latest in high-tech combat gear.

The floor displays included a Bradley MICV sitting in a roped-off area as groups of visitors inspected its array of bristling weapons. Elsewhere in the vast exhibition hall, a Huey Blackhawk chopper was under scrutiny, as were a HUMVEE High Mobility Vehicle and a Commando APC.

Each visitor to the show wore plastic ID tags. The show was an industry affair, and the public, although openly admitted, was not encouraged to attend.

Zabriskie and Domino were each handed visitor tags at the reception desk behind the plate-glass entrance doors. Z-Comm's resident pretty boy had charmed the beautiful merc into accompanying him to the exhibition.

Although an acquaintance of Zabriskie had a booth at the show, Zabriskie's main interest was in keeping in touch with developments in the field. As an independent consultant who built special-order gear for a select clientele, Zabriskie liked to see what the competition was up to.

But the scion of a wealthy family wasn't in it for the money. He had plenty. Zabriskie didn't need to risk his ass in clandestine fire-zones either, just as he hadn't needed to sign up for a second tour in Nam. Like many others from his social circle, he could have gone to a shrink and been 4F'd out of the war to begin with.

But like his Z-Comm pards, Harry Zabriskie was a man with a monkey on his back. He fed that monkey by taking crazy risks. It was the way he'd always lived and, yeah, the way he'd probably die.

Heads turned as he and Domino moved through the cluster of men in business suits eyeballing the assortment of hardware on display.

The lady merc had the kind of cold beauty that attracted attention anywhere. She was an ice queen in a world of gnomes, fairies, and dwarves, an archetypal dragon lady.

The booth they were headed for was sandwiched between two others. The one on the left belonged to a company that manufactured silencers for small arms; the one on the right had an array of military commo gear on display.

"Strewth! If it ain't old Harry!"

The guy behind the closest booth waved Zabriskie over. He was a tall, slim Australian with a receding hairline and a hollow-cheeked face. Zabriskie and he had served together in the Nam. The logo behind him read Slater Military Electronics. Sophisticated long-range communications equipment was on the table in front of him. Ross Slater wouldn't win any beauty contents, but the Aussie outshone everybody else when it came to inventing viciously clever scrambling devices.

Slater's company specialized in debugging, both for government and private industry.

Zabriskie pumped Slater's hand.

"Who's the bird, mate?" Slater asked, his moist, doglike brown eyes devouring Domino.

"Ross," Zabriskie said, putting his arm around Domino's shoulders. "Let me introduce you to the future Mrs. Harry Zabriskie, Mona Greenblatt of French Lick, Indiana." Zabriskie grinned toothily at Domino, who glared back. "Mona and I plan to be married next month. We've already picked out a dream house in Denver."

Slater kept staring at Domino with a carnivorous gleam in his sunken brown eyes. "Congratulations," he said. "Harry's a fair dinkum bloke. I'm sure you'll be as happy together as two koala bears in a billibong tree."

Zabriskie squeezed Domino's shoulders. "We already are," he said. "Isn't that right, darling?"

"Up yours, Zabriskie," she said.

Zabriskie laughed.

" 'Up yours, Zabriskie,' she said. Isn't she a riot? What a sense of humor. That's what I love about Mona. Her sense of humor."

Ross suddenly looked over Zabriskie's shoulder. An angry look came over his face.

"Flippin' bloody drongo!" he shouted. "Here come the ruddy cobbers again."

A moment later, three guys in badly fitting suits crowded around Slater's booth. They had broad smiles plastered on their swarthy faces. The warts and bushy mustaches were a dead giveaway.

"Please to give brochure with full specifications on SCR-2700 semiautomatic receiver system," one of the newcomers said in a Russian accent as thick as his mustache.

Slater flailed his long, spidery arms.

"I told you Soviet fart-suckers to piss off before," he bellowed. "I'll ruddy call flippin' security." He looked around. "Strewth! Where in the bloody chromo's security?"

"Please to give brochure with full specifications on SCR-2700 semiautomatic receiver system," the same guy said to Slater with the identical broad smile plastered on his face.

"Look, I told you ruddy damned borscht puking—"

Slater stopped in midsentence.

The Russian suddenly had no face.

It had disintegrated into a free-form sculpture made of raw hamburger. One of the Russian's eyes spurted out in a jet of blood, struck the center of Slater's high forehead, and ran down his right cheek.

A pulsebeat later, the headless corpse went into convulsions, flopping across the table with an ugly crashing sound as the high-end commo gear was thrown to the floor.

"Time to slip another shrimp on the barbie, mate," Slater shouted to Zabriskie as he dove for cover. "Hooroo, jackeroo!"

Two regulation-sized hardmen in dark suits were standing with Ingram MAC 10s at hip level, cranking out deadly fire as complacently as if they were handing out business cards.

The black sound-suppressor cones that projected from the boxlike receivers of the SMGs reduced the reports of the rapidly ejected .45 ACP slugs to a series of low-decibel spits.

Empty attache cases from which the silenced hardware had been pulled moments before lay at the feet of the triggermen, discarded as the blitz went down.

Pushing Domino ahead, Zabriskie dodged to the armored MICV on display nearby, hunkering beside the war wagon as a stream of silenced autofire whispered overhead before thudding into a wall and leaving behind a zigzag of bulletholes.

"Shit," Zabriskie remarked, "they'll let anybody in nowadays."

Telling Domino to stay put behind the MICV, Zabriskie dodged MAC fire in a daredevil leap that brought him rolling across the display board and into the booth beside Slater's.

Weapons, silencers, and ammo mags fell over him with a tinny clatter that was music to Zabriskie's ears. Music second only to the sound that the Z-Commando's answering fire would make. Zabriskie fisted a Mini-Uzi subgun and checked the weapon's 32-round clip.

The box magazine was filled with 9-mm parabellums. He unthreaded the black tube of the Uzi's silencer and jammed the weapon into the back of his pants.

Snatching up an Ingram MAC 11, he made certain that it had a full clip too.

Zabriskie also stuffed as many spare magazines for both weapons as he could carry into his pockets.

"Catch!" he hollered at Domino, pitching her the lightweight yet lethal .380 caliber SMG. "The clip's full of live ones."

Domino studded the select-fire lever of the Mini MAC into full-auto mode and pulled out its wire buttstock. Zabriskie whipped out the Uzi and propped it over the top of the display board, sighting through the Israeli subgun's barleycorn sights.

The hitguys had vanished.

"Goddammit!" Zabriskie swore, cautiously looking around. "Where'd they go?"

There was no time to stick around waiting for trouble to reappear, though. And the Z-Commandos couldn't afford to assume that the opposition had just up and walked away.

Domino cautiously moved from the MICV at a low crouch. The Ingram SMG in her hand waved back and forth in a horizontal arc as her ice-blue eyes tracked each section of the firezone.

Flanking her, Zabriskie moved fast. Clutching the Uzi in a two-handed combat stance, he whipped the muzzle from side to side, ready for immediate target acquisition at the slightest sign of lethal threat.

Pfutt! Pfutttt! Pfuttttttt!

The muffled reports of the more slowly cycling MAC 10s as they rotored out the heavier .45 ACP rivets was followed by the whine of slugs ricocheting off in a hundred directions.

The Z-Commandos tracked on the noise-suppressed bursts as best they could as they dodged behind an LTV High Mobility Vehicle. The faint twinkle of the MACs from an observation level above told them that the hitters had climbed to the second tier of the arena for a better shot.

From there they controlled the entire field below. The hardgunners could turn the show area into a slaughterhouse. No problem.

To make matters worse, the backup snuff crew of full-auto blasters had just entered the arena through the main gate. They were armed with AKMs spitting out 7.62-mm heavies. Zabriskie and Domino were caught in a double bind.

Sliding toward the cab, Zabriskie saw that the show functionary who had been moving the HUMVEE was slumped to one side. A stray round had creased his temple. He was unconscious, though otherwise unhurt. Zabriskie jumped into the passenger side. The keys to the vehicle were already in the ignition.

Zabriskie rolled the driver out of the HUMVEE as gently as he could and slid behind the wheel through the passenger-side door. Domino climbed in and used the MAC 11 to lay down what suppressing fire she could as Zabriskie started up the engine.

In low gear, the HUMVEE took off across the show area toward the plate-glass doors of the entrance, gathering speed as it rolled. Zabriskie shifted into third as a brace of 7.62-mm bullets shattered the rear windshield of the military workhorse vehicle.

Shifting into overdrive, Zabriskie plowed the HUMVEE through the arena's plate-glass entrance doors and was out into the broad plaza that surrounded the C.I.P. Convention Center.

Passersby scattered for cover as the war wagon screamed through the doors in a blizzard of shattering glass and bumped over the uneven surface of the cobbled plaza before its heavy tires grabbed asphalt again on one of the broad streets than ran nearby.

In the sideview mirror, Zabriskie could see the opposition run like hell toward two Citroens that had pulled up in front of the Convention Center entrance and climb inside.

The Citroens took off after the HUMVEE in a hell of a hurry, gunfire blazing from their rolled-down windows.

FIVE

Some sixth sense warned Proffit.

He wheeled around in time to catch the two newcomers to the art gallery whipping compact black subguns from beneath their windbreakers and bringing the blasters into snuff position.

Before the deadly duo could unleash razoring steel from combat crouches, Proffit moved with swift, homicidal precision.

The Z-Commando didn't have any firearms at hand.

But then again, he didn't need any.

Proffit's uncanny ability to turn virtually any object into a lethal weapon—including his fists and his feet—had astonished team-mate and antagonist alike on numerous occasions.

It was an ability refined and sharpened by Colonel Logan Cage years before in the jungles of Vietnam. With Proffit as his one-man death squad, the leader of the Special Operations Group, SAD/COSM, had effectively turned the VC's own dirty tricks against them, usually with a couple of even dirtier variations thrown in to add insult to injury.

On a black marble pedestal beside Proffit stood a winglike arc of brushed chrome titled "Phoenix." Proffit grabbed the heavy piece of sculpture from its base and hurled it like a boomerang in one swift, fluid motion.

The movement had been instantaneous and unpremeditated. Proffit had reacted without wasted thought or movement. Like the Zen archers of Japan, he was able to aim the sculpture with the accuracy of a guided missile. A wrist flick sent it spinning on its lethal trajectory.

The brushed-steel boomerang whirled across the gallery with astonishing speed and deadly precision. The 30-pound sculptural work slammed with piledriving force into the gun hand of one SMG shooter, crushing the metacarpals to useless pulp.

The Ingram flew from his grasp, clattering as it slid across the polished marble floor of the gallery, and the hardman windmilled backward with an animal howl.

Behind the injured goon was a sculpture bristling with spikes of steel, titled "Happy Valley '68." The sculpture was a realistic model of a Viet Cong booby trap. Fashioned of brushed stainless steel, it was designed to function as lethally as the original that had inspired it.

Blood fountained from the gunman's chest in a dozen places as he tumbled backward and was impaled on the rows of gleaming steel pungi stakes, each honed to vicious razorpoints. The enforcer's body went into convulsions before his back arched and he fell back with a bloody gurgle against the bed of spikes.

Although momentarily stunned by the swift termination of their beefy pard, the other three shootists recovered and, balancing on the balls of their feet, snapped their autopistols back up, trying to draw a bead on their target before he pulled any more slick, deadly moves.

Proffit used the precious seconds he'd bought to push Penny to safety behind a massive sculpture made of welded steel I-beams and barbed wire called "M.I.A."

By the time the hitmen got him back in their sights, Proffit had already disappeared into the corridor beyond the gallery room.

Okay, thought Proffit to himself as he sprinted across the corridor. *Game time.*

Out of the Mardi Gras meltdown but up against a second death squad of AKM-packing terrorists, Cage and Bear had no choice at all but to duck into the cover of a nearby hotel.

The hotel lobby was packed with party

animals, most of them thoroughly shitfaced. It seemed like the entire city of Rio was on a massive bender tonight. Behind Cage and Bear, the AKM-packing uglies sprinted into the air-conditioned ground-floor level.

This hit crew wore face masks.

Duck masks.

Anyplace else, the bizarre game of tag would have attracted immediate attention. In the pandemonium of the celebration, though, nobody noticed another bunch of drunken crazies hightailing it through the thronged bodies for who-knows-what reason. The few people that looked their way immediately assumed that the dangerously real autoweapons were harmless water guns.

Cage and MacBeth cut through the lobby into a disco, ignoring the little guy who was sitting at the ticket stand by the entrance. Revolving mirror globes overhead cast whirling flecks of light over them as they elbowed through the crowded dance floor. Strobe lights made them appear to move in Chaplinesque slow motion.

Although it was nearly one A.M., the dancers gyrated with a manic determination to the sound of a megawatt stereo system cranking out a Bee Gees' tune with Spanish lyrics, looking like they were capable of partying just as hard till sunup.

Scantily clad women and men bumped and ground their tanned, sweaty bodies against one another to the overtly sexual music booming and blaring over the amplified sound system.

"Vengamos! A partiron a nosotros!"

A woman with a painted face and black hair garlanded with tropical flowers jumped on Cage. With amazing agility, she locked her arms around his back and her legs around his butt and jammed her sweaty, large-nippled breasts into his face.

A guy wearing a devil's mask that ended in a phallic green Day-Glo nose began hollering something in Spanish. Cage didn't understand the patter but the message was clear. He untangled the woman with as much difficulty as if she were a human leech.

"Wassamatta," she asked him with a Spanish accent, "you no like girls?"

"Only the good parts," Cage returned and pushed past the clinging Brazilian vine.

Another woman, wearing only a black G-string, her slender body glistening with fragrant oil, hopped on Bear's back. She poured a pitcher of ice-cold beer over his bald head. A laughing man in a Santa Claus suit handed her another pitcher.

"Hey, fuck that," Bear hollered. He grabbed the pitcher of brew and downed it in one long gulp that was followed by an even longer burp.

They finally managed to shove and bull their way across the jam-packed dance floor of hardcore party animals and out one of the exit doors, just a hop-skip-and-jump ahead of the cartoon-masked gun crew behind them. The exit door led to the kitchen beyond the disco, and as Bear crashed through the swinging door, he and Cage bowled over a waiter carrying a tray heaped with plates of food.

The waiter shouted at the two crazy gringos as they dashed past him into the huge kitchen area. Cooks in starched white uniforms dropped what they were doing and stared goggle-eyed. A couple were even brandishing knives and meat cleavers as the two maniacs barreled past them, knocking over cutlery and cookware in a blaring cacophony of crashing metal and shattering china.

A pair of duck-masked blasters were through the doors immediately after them. Bear and Cage tried to draw a bead on the opposition, but there was no way to fire without hitting a good guy in the confusion. Bear opted to do the next best thing. If he couldn't throw lead, then he'd throw a little stainless steel. Cutlery, that is.

Grabbing a meat cleaver he sent it on a propellering end-over-end trajectory toward the closest duck-masked fucker behind them. The rotoring cleaver scored a direct hit right between the eyes, splitting his skull open like an overripe grapefruit. Cage picked up an empty garbage can and sent it rolling at the surviving duck men, who jumped back across surrounding tables to avoid getting bowled over.

The diversion worked so well that Cage and Bear decided to follow it up by throwing pots, pans, more garbage cans, and whatever else they could lay their hands on behind them as they hustled out of the kitchen, then down a cinderblock-walled, fluorescent-lit corridor that dead-ended at a metal fire exit.

Autofire chattered as Cage and Bear reached the door. Whirling, Bear cut loose with a SPAS blast while Cage launched a controlled 9-mm Uzi burst at the two duckface gunners who were firing their automatic pistols from combat crouches. Bullets whined as they ricocheted off the cinderblocks, and the duck shooters ducked for cover.

Hitting the emergency exit's crash bar and throwing open the door, Cage and Bear ran outside again. A floodlit parking lot surrounded by a low perimeter fence loomed in front of them, deserted in the humid tropical night. While Cage snicked open a Black Finger spring knife and cut dashboard cables to hotwire the ignition of a car they'd found with an unlocked door, MacBeth cut loose with a SPAS-16 burst that blew away one of the hardguys as the kill crew exited from the hotel emergency exit behind them.

Hearing the motor come alive, MacBeth jumped into the car. He and Cage careened out of the parking lot dodging a hail of autofire from the surviving shootist.

Something told them that they'd either have to cut their visit short or let somebody do it for them.

SIX

Zabriskie piloted the hijacked HUMVEE through the mazelike streets of central Paris. Before the HUMVEE had gotten a quarter mile from the exhibition hall off the Champs Elysees, the local police had joined in the high-speed car chase. Now both the *flic* and the shooters were on the Z-crew's trail.

A few streets ahead, rush hour traffic was gridlocked at the Place de l'Etoile, the monster traffic circle surrounding the Arc de Triomphe that pinwheels out in a dozen directions.

Zabriskie stopped the HUMVEE and he and Domino left it where it stood in the middle of a traffic lane. It wasn't about to take them any further. They hotfooted it down Avenue Kleber to the accompaniment of motorists blaring their horns and cussing them out in French, cut across more grid-locked cars on the Place du Trocadero, and headed into the treelined walkways surrounding the Place de Chaillot.

Behind the Z-Commandos, the cops and the terror crew followed suit, spilling out of the chase cars and taking off after the two fleeing Americans on foot.

The terrorist hit crew in the Citroen had a good five-minute lead on the cops, though. Its heavily armed passengers were right behind Zabriskie and Domino as they bee-lined it across a small bridge over the Seine toward the Eiffel Tower.

There was a crowd of people there, sight-seers and locals both, and they figured they could get lost in the crush of the crowd.

With their weapons almost dry, they'd stand no chance in a firefight, and they were bound to come up losers whether they got nailed by the terror crew or pinched by the cops.

Zabriskie paid the small admission fee and he and Domino joined the crowd of sight-seers that was making its way to the tower. Looking behind them, they saw that the chase crew was a few dozen yards back, shouldering through the crowd. This wasn't going to work.

"Come on," Zabriskie yelled, spotting an entrance to the Paris Metro. Domino and he both ran past the throng of riders lined up at the ticket booth and jumped the turnstiles.

They hustled down a flight of stairs, deaf to the shouts of uniformed ticket-sellers behind them.

A train was pulling into the station, strangely noiseless on its rubber wheels, a fact that made the Paris Metro different from any other subway system in the world. Zabriskie and Domino got onboard. As the doors closed, two of the hardmen managed to shove their way into one of the cars farther down the platform. They weren't more than two cars behind them when the train began pulling out again.

The train was an express train. As it slid into the tunnel and picked up speed between the Eiffel Tower stop and the Place de l'Opera station, the hitters began elbowing through the crowded subway car.

As soon as the express pulled into its next stop, Zabriskie and Domino got off in a hurry. They now found themselves in a rabbit warren of tile-walled tunnels. Passengers weaved in all directions, oblivious to the game of terminal tag being played in their midst.

Exiting the train behind them, the hardmen decided not to waste any more shoe leather, and started blasting away with SMG fire as the conductor slid the doors closed behind them. Zabriskie and Domino rolled to either side as a fragburst cut down a man in a business suit, blowing his head off in midstride.

A woman screamed. Up and down the

platform, passengers hit the ground, dove behind garbage cans, and took cover anywhere they could.

Hunkering behind two large trash bins, the Z-Commandos returned fire, using up their remaining ammo supply in a few short bursts.

Short, but effective.

Zabriskie's SMG salvo blew a badass shooter back against the train at which he crouched, gripping his SMG in a two-handed combat stance as he raked the platform with blazing fire. He wound up in a sitting position, half his belly on the deck in front of him. The surviving two hardmen bolted to either side of their checked-off pard.

One of them held his SMG to the conductor's head and forced him to reopen the train's doors. The shooters darted inside. Smashing the windows, they cut loose with a fresh spray of bullets.

A crew of gendarmes suddenly appeared from a feeder tunnel that led onto the platform. They opened up on the gummen, eyeballing the shooters without spotting Zabriskie and Domino.

The Z-Commandos let the cops and the terrorists battle it out. Dropping their weapons into the trash bins as unobtrusively as they were able, they elbowed their way through the crowd of Frog rubberneckers who thronged the passageways of the Metro station watching the firefight, and escaped to street level in the confusion.

They hailed a taxi topside on the Boulevard Haussmann and took it to Zabriskie's hotel in the 17th arrondissement. The cabbie, recognizing their American accents, asked in Gallic-accented English, "What goes on down there? More terrorists, I bet you."

"We don't know," Zabriskie returned. "All we know is that we don't want any trouble. We're on our honeymoon, you see. Scott and Zelda Fitzgerald from Des Moines, Iowa."

The driver nodded his head.

"Very bad, these terrorists," he told them. "Especially for young people who are in the love, no?"

"Yeah," Zabriskie said, adding, "and to add insult to injury, somebody picked our pockets and stole all our credit cards and travelers checks."

"You have the American Express?" asked the driver.

"Yeah," Zabriskie returned with a smile. "Good thing we didn't leave home without it."

A jagged line of bulletholes stitched a Rembrandt canvas, destroying a priceless masterpiece beyond all hope of repair.

Slug fragments whined and spanged off the museum's polished terra-cotta floor and shattered the bulbs in the rows of overhead light fixtures.

A sculpture by Picasso was permanently defaced by a line of pockmarks up and down its length, although its appearance was only improved by the addition of the holes.

Sam Proffit skidded on the treacherously smooth marble as he rounded the corner of the gallery. Chips of plaster knocked loose by a slug that narrowly missed his head stung the side of his neck.

The hit crew was on him like stink on shit, and suddenly there was a guard directly in front of him. Seeing trouble but not understanding what was going down, the guy did the predictable. He clawed at the .38 Police Special holstered at his side.

His eyes were on Proffit with the unmistakable look of a small mind making a bad call. If Proffit allowed the guard to bring the revolver into firing position, his life wasn't worth a pisshole in the snow.

If the guard stopped him now, the snuff detail behind him would perforate them both. If Proffit refused to stop when the guard hollered "freeze," then odds were that the trigger-happy cop would blow him into the Astral Plane.

Proffit hated to do it, but he had to stop the guard before his bad call on the tense situation got them both killed.

Ducking low, Proffit sent the rent-a-cop into dreamland with a thrust kick to the solar plexus. He'd be sore for a couple of weeks, but it was better than being laid out on a morgue slab for the rest of eternity.

As tempting as it was, though, Proffit had no time to duck and make a grab for the guard's dropped .38 Special. By the time he had the weapon cocked and aimed at his pursuers, a brace of whirlwinding hollow-points would have turned him into cream of merc.

Instead of dipping for sucker bait, Proffit hightailed it down the corridor without missing a beat. He'd have to either take the fuckers out without weapons or get away clean.

From where Proffit stood, both choices looked like no-shows. He could tell that these dudes weren't throwaways. They were pros. This meant that the hit had been well-planned. Backup would be waiting in the wings. For shit and sure.

Proffit's mind whirled as he crunched numbers and computed the survival options.

"There goes the skinny fucker!" he heard one of the goons holler from the entrance to another wing of the museum just up ahead. *"You're history, douche-bag! That was my brother you iced back there!"* As happened so often in life, the opposition had already made the decision for him.

The backup crew's appearance on scene meant that he was now boxed between the two extermination teams, caught like a fly in a pisspot.

Proffit had no choice but to dodge down the stairwell a few paces up ahead and to his right and shag it down to the next level. He didn't want to attempt to reach the main floor because it would be swarming with guards who would probably wind up acting as a de facto firing squad.

The exhibit hall one floor down was closed to the public for renovations. Although light from a parallel corridor spilled into it, the room was in semi-darkness. Despite the gloom, Proffit could see that he was now in a section of the museum dealing with the medieval period.

Suits of armor stood in ranks along one side of the large, high-ceilinged room. Glass display cases were filled with medieval instruments of bloody mayhem. There were lances, pikes, broadswords, javelins, maces, battleaxes, and other crude but lethal man-killers on exhibit under glass.

An elbow smash, and a broadsword was missing from its stand and in Proffit's hands.

Clutching the sword, he squatted behind another display case nearby and waited for his playmates to put in an appearance. The hitguys appeared at the entrance to the exhibit hall right on cue. Like the pros they were, they pulled up short and assumed positions bracketing the entranceway before they risked an ambush on entering the darkened exhibit hall.

Proffit dipped into his fancy sportjacket and flipped a handful of change across the hard marble floor. It might have been the oldest trick in the book, but then again, it hadn't earned that reputation because it failed to produce results.

Before the crew boss, who knew better, could stop his three simian flunkies, both snapped bursts of fire in the direction of the sudden jingling sound and dazzle of motion. Not only did Proffit's gambit divert the blasting party's attention, but the sudden muzzle flash gave away the position of two knuckle-draggers now in the exhibit hall with him.

Suddenly on his feet, Proffit hurled the nearby broadsword at the MAC gunner to the far right of the scum quartet with all his might.

The sword plunged clean through the guy's upper abdomen and sank to the hilt in the drywall behind him, harpooning the hitter like an ugly species of poisonous eel and creating a brand-new exhibit.

Blood belched in thick gouts from his nostrils and mouth as he frantically tried to yank the sword out of his abdomen before his body went into a terminal seizure. Then he suddenly went limp and sagged like a bloody puppet, one hand swinging back and forth and sprinkling the floor with his blood.

That left three more of the opposition still breathing—one outside and two inside the semi-darkened exhibition hall with him pointing .45 ACP Ingrams.

Suddenly the room lights came on. The man outside had smarts enough to look for the switching box. Proffit shielded his eyes as the medieval gallery was bathed in dazzling brilliance. Although concealed behind a display case, he was no longer as well hidden as he'd been in the shadows of the dark exhibit hall moments before. They were pros, all right.

"Listen up, cocksucker!" the hit team's leader man hollered. "Here's the real deal."

Proffit heard the metallic crack of a spent clip being ejected and a new one snapped crisply into the receiver of an SMG to one side as he crouched on the balls of his feet behind the display case.

Next came another sound, one that made Proffit's blood turn to ice in his veins.

"That sound you just heard was the cotter pin of a fragmentation grenade being pulled from the spoon," the gravel-voiced shooter went on. "I'll give you until the count of three to haul ass over here or I pitch the grenade. It's your call, candyass."

Proffit stood up from behind the display case. The two guys inside the hall were regulation-size scum soldiers. Both were big, rawboned types with square faces and pug noses. Two clutched SMGs, and from the way they held them, knew how to use the auto-weapons. The third man held the pineapple. True to his word, Proffit saw that the cotter pin was missing.

"You're smart," the lead hardguy said as the two mouth-breathers who bracketed him stepped closer to Proffit. "Now gimme the rest of the drill." One of the slope-browed brackets jerked the SMG barrel sharply up.

Proffit shot his hands over his head.

The grenade-waver stepped closer, the muzzle of the MAC ready to fire. "Don't try anything funny, babycakes," he said with a heavy Southern drawl. "This lickin' stick's got a hair trigger." The dude's breath was the direct opposite of kissing-sweet. Unless you happened to be a blue bottle fly, that is.

"Hey, no problem," Proffit said. Suddenly he sidestepped, tucking left.

The hardman's eyes widened in fear as he saw death coming straight at him. But there was nothing he could do.

Except, of course, die.

The crossbow Proffit had rigged to fire when he tripped the ultra-thin filament stretched from the trigger to the leg of a display case sent the iron bolt whizzing across the hall. He'd made the tripwire by pulling the seams out of his new jacket. At least now he didn't feel like such a wimp about letting Penny railroad him into wearing it.

The bolt was aimed perfectly.

It pierced the grenade-holder's Adam's apple and came out through the back of his neck.

The crude dude dropped his grenade and clawed desperately at the shaft protruding from his trachea while his eyes bugged in his head and blood gushered madly from the second mouth that had opened up below his jawline.

He actually managed to pull out the bolt, and stared stupidly at it with blood jetting thickly from his ruptured throat.

Proffit rolled away from the stricken hitter

and grabbed for the first kill's MAC lying on the gleaming terra-cotta floor of the gallery an instant before the grenade exploded.

Proffit sucked floor, MAC in hand. Cordite smoke and clouds of pulverized plaster filled the room. Somewhere in that cloud were the two surviving Cro-Magnons who had leap-frogged from the blast zone a moment before the grenade went off.

A pulsebeat later, there were bullets singing a funeral dirge all around him as Proffit rolled behind a display case and came up clutching the MAC with a fresh clip of .45 ACP manshredders in its handgrip.

A stream of purifying hellfire lanced out like a glittering Reaper's blade at the hard-gunner stationed nearest the exhibit hall's entrance.

The death stream caught the bushwhacker across the chest in an ugly diagonal slash of rupturing red holes and he instantly donated a couple of pints of blood to the floor below him. Another burst wounded Proffit's last antagonist high in the gut.

Autofire raked the walls and ceiling as death spasms triggered a wild burst from the MAC's muzzle and the first hardguy did a kind of Indian rain dance, stumbled sideways into a display case, and pitched over at a crazy angle. Crashing into a wall, the ventilated hitter knocked loose a collection of mounted battleaxes and spears that buried him under a heap of wood and metal.

He was already dead but nothing had

bothered to tell his brainstem that. Caught in its final moments as the heart muscle died, the primitive core of his consciousness desperately fired mad signals at its limbs, causing them to thrash with demented fury.

Proffit aimed the MAC at the dead man's head and blew it to muck with a mercy burst.

Something struck him on the back.

Snearing pain blossomed in his mind.

Proffit turned to see a snarling bloody thing wildly clawing at him. The surviving hardguy who'd been hit in the gut had slammed the spiked head of a mace into Proffit's shoulder.

The guy was big and as strong as a bull. He had a long way to go yet before he went to rat heaven. Before he checked out, he was out to punch Proffit's ticket too.

The impact knocked Proffit's SMG from his grasp. It tumbled clattering to the marble floor and slid out of reach beneath a display case.

The creep had Proffit down. He raised the mace over his head, gripping its handle with both hands, and with a savage bellow, prepared to bring it crashing down on his prone victim's stomach.

Proffit dodged away a microinstant before the spiked ball of iron slammed into the floor. The ancient spikes forged for battle centuries before became embedded in the terra-cotta floor by the crushing force of the killer blow.

As the gut-shot creep strained to yank the

mace free, Proffit pivoted and launched a high side kick at the guy's ribcage.

He felt the satisfying shatter of bone and cartilage as the kick connected with the soft tissue inside his chest cavity and drove razor-edged splinters into his heart and lungs. All it did, though, was send the guy crashing to one knee.

Bleeding like a slaughtered ox but still very much alive, he turned and charged Proffit with his head down. Proffit sidestepped the last-ditch death lunge and kicked the crudbag in the tailbone, sending him flying head-first into a display panel.

Mounted on the wall above him was an enormous iron mantrap from Sixteenth Century England. The impact jarred the mantrap loose from its mount, and as the guy pulled his head from the busted panel, it fell over him and snapped shut.

The dead hitter's body pitched over, minus one head. The head lay inside the iron jaws of the trap on the floor beside him.

SEVEN

Less than a week after the bloody shootouts between Z-Comm and the scum brigades of Terrorist International, the strike team had assembled in Paris to be briefed by Peter Quartermaine.

The multiple assassination attempts on the members of Z-Command showed the telltale signs of a payback blitz. But the motive behind the coordinated snuff attempts was still unclear.

Quartermaine—Z-Comm's liaison with government and private clients who contracted the merc crew for suicide runs that would make members of glory outfits like Delta Force crap in their camos—confirmed that the Mad Dog of the Middle East, Muammar Qaddafi, had personally ordered out the strikers as a quid pro quo for the anti-terrorist op inside Libya.

But there was more going on than just violent retaliation for a commando raid that made Daffy Qaddafi lose face among the low-life leaders of fifteenth-rate shitholes in the Third World.

The overall picture, Cage learned as he met Quartermaine on the Quai D'Orsay—which paralleled the Left Bank of the foul-smelling River Seine—to get brought up to date, was starting to have more twists and turns than a barrel full of eels.

"We've learned that Qaddafi was tipped to your identities through sources in the Chadian military," Quartermaine began. "That's the Chadians' problem and they're pissed as all hell. The leak will be found and when he is, he'll get justice the way it's practiced in that part of the world—fast and final."

Quartermaine lit up one of his trademark Rijtmeester panatellas and leaned against the ancient stone parapet between the cobbled Quai surface and the swiftly rushing currents of the river below. It was late on a gray afternoon, and the sky was a mass of leaden clouds that bulged against the Parisian roofscape. The city of Paris looked old and hunched beneath the gunmetal-colored sky, a sad-sack whore who had long ago outlived the glamor days of her glittering youth.

"The key to getting a fix on why the colonel

wanted your balls for bookends lies in understanding the mission that the terror crew was training for at the time you whacked them out," Quartermaine went on, exhaling curling streams of thick white smoke through his nostrils.

"Interrogation of the two prisoners helo'd to Ouadi Doum revealed that they were an elite team being prepared for a special assignment in the U.S. and Europe.

"The team was handpicked from a pool of international volunteers. Its training involved the deployment of CBW weapons against major targets. Washington, New York, London, Rome. The strikers were to suicide-out once they'd accomplished their missions. The plan was to launch the biggest and most ambitious terror strike ever undertaken."

"Where would Qaddafi get his hands on chemical-biologicals?" Cage asked.

"That's where we got hit with the punchline," Quartermaine returned. "The CBW agents come from Hitler's Germany."

Cage leaned over the polished stone parapet and watched a sleek tour boat glide upriver toward the Eiffel Tower, its decks filled with rubberneckers listening to a guide point out the sights over a public-address system.

"As you know, after Berlin fell to the Allies in April, 1945, Europe was thrown into complete chaos," Quartermaine continued. "The Nazi brass fell over each other trying to cut separate deals with the Allies once they heard that their fearless leader had punched his own ticket in his command bunker beneath Berlin. Some of them eventually did wind up cutting deals. Those who were able to offer what the Allies were shopping for."

"Operation Paperclip," Cage returned, still watching the tour boat. "The Nazi scientists like Von Braun given a no-questions-asked ticket to the States in return for services rendered."

It had gone even further than that, Cage knew. Long after the war had ended the CIA continued to keep former Nazi intelligence networks in Europe in place. The personnel were former German Abwehr spooks. The only difference now was the color of the money they were paid with. When the public began asking questions, the so-called Nazi "ratline" was set up to ship the goose-steppers to South America where they would hopefully vanish into the jungle, never to be heard from again.

"Exactly. London and Washington on the one side and the Soviets on the other knew the Nazis were years ahead of the Allies in certain areas of technology. They were only a few months behind us in the development of a nuclear bomb. They were on the verge of developing a crude yet effective ICBM technology. There are even reliable reports of a German flying saucer that was seen by eyewitnesses months prior to the conclusion of the war. And the Krauts had already developed the first operational jet fighter of the twentieth century."

Both men watched a young Parisienne in a plastic miniskirt walk past, her butt swinging like a metronome as she disappeared down into a Metro station. A group of boys walked past, one of them carrying a boom box that blared a Jim Morrison tune that had been big on the jukeboxes at Cam Ranh Bay before the Frenchies had even been born.

"For a lot of the brass stranded in eastern Europe after Berlin fell, there was the choice of either getting captured by the American side or falling into Russian hands. Who wanted to chase borscht with vodka for the rest of their lives? Entire German divisions tried to fight their way over to Allied territory; they knew what the Soviets would do to them.

"One of those columns was a crew of SS Werewolves. They were mostly kids at the time, the most fanatic and dangerous of the Hitler Youth. The Werewolves formed the nucleus of postwar Nazi paramilitary forces."

"And they were practically all that was still left of Nazi reserve troops by that time," Cage added.

"Affirmative. This particular bunch came out of the Nordhausen testing grounds, a huge underground complex in southeastern

Germany. The guy in charge was a Nazi named Hans Kleist, formerly assigned to the Treblinka extermination camp. Kleist knew he needed a card to play with the Americans. He assembled a cache of the most sophisticated weapons they were working on, complete with all the pertinent files. His intention was to trade that weapons cache for his life and the lives of his men.

"But like so many others, Kleist's men never made it to Allied lines. Partisans encircled them and massacred most of them through sheer force of numbers. Kleist and a small band of his fanatically loyal SS troops managed to hide the weapons cache and punch through the partisan death cordon. Kleist then dropped out of sight.

"Twenty years later, though, the Israeli Mossad tracked Kleist to Panama and Argentina, where he was a high-ranking member of *Die Spinne* or The Spider, the Nazi brotherhood that takes care of the survivors of the Third Reich. The cache of weapons squirreled away by Kleist's men were never located."

Cage flipped his cigaret over the embankment of the ancient quay and into the gunmetal waters of the polluted river. He watched another tour boat glide lazily past, this one downriver. The strains of tinny music drifted up, puncutated by the sound of high-pitched laughter and a female guide's amplified voice over the public-address system.

"A couple of months ago," Quartermaine went on, "Kleist vanished from Panama. The Israeli Mossad was interested. If they could grab him outside of Latin America, then maybe they could pull an Eichmann-style snatch.

"But the old fox was as wily as ever. The Mossad men lost him somewhere in Europe. Then we got lucky, sort of. An American on a business trip to Amsterdam, a former inmate of one of the death camps that Kleist used as a source of experimental subjects, spotted the guy in a cafe on the Ledseplein in Amsterdam. The guy must have been made because somebody blew him away shortly after he ID'd Kleist, although not before he reported spotting Kleist to the U.S. embassy there."

A NATO F-111 shrieked past in the direction of Montmarte as clouds bunched together overhead, further darkening the afternoon sky. The tour boat slipped around a bend in the river and disappeared from view beyond the Ile St. Louis. A middle-aged American tourist couple sat down at a cafe table and were joined by a black street gypsy who was chased away by one of the waiters. A forked tongue of lightning flicked across the sky. Thunder rolled across the City of Light.

"Nobody knows why Kleist broke from cover. Maybe he needed money. Maybe he was just tired of bananaland. Who knows? What we strongly suspect is that Kleist's trip abroad was to confirm the location of the hidden technology cache after more than forty years of hiding. This dovetails neatly with the Apocalypse Battalion's training program in Libya. Qaddafi would pay a king's ransom for the Nazi bugs."

"Crude but effective weapons," Cage offered. "Qaddafi's done it before. Most of the world supply of plastic explosive for terrorist use was sold to the colonel by a disgruntled spook with access to the C-4. The prospect of laying hands on some cut-rate bugs would probably make the Mad Dog foam at the mouth."

"Exactly," Quartermaine responded. "Why fuck around with anything sophisticated? Bugs are bugs. The old Nazi stuff can kill you just as dead. And he can get it from Kleist at bargain-basement prices. With added bonuses from whatever else is in the cache to sweeten the deal."

Both men straightened up. The sun was beginning to set behind the Eiffel Tower. A group of schoolchildren raced past, taunting each other in rapid and unintelligible Parisian street language. An ambulance siren shrieked high-low, high-low as it raced past on the Boulevard des Invalides behind them.

"What's the status of the cache now?" Cage asked.

Quartermaine squinted at the Parisian

skyline etched in black against the red ball of the setting sun as it slid into darkness.

"That's what that chickenshit outfit of yours is about to find out."

EIGHT

Forty-five years after the Proteus Chain had been crated and hidden, the collection of Nazi bioweapons was again ready to be sold to the highest bidder. A vintage death brew, it would command a high price from the connoisseurs of the wine of revolution who savored its lethal bouquet.

The swastika-emblazoned canisters of deadly biological agents were now secure in foam-cushioned aluminum hardboxes.

All week long, representatives of Third World republics had come and gone to inspect the goods on the terrorist auction block and put in their bids.

Operatives of Iran, Iraq, Cuba, Angola, and a dozen other despotic regimes looking for an edge in the petty wars and territorial squabbles that were their timeless obsessions had beaten a path to Kleist's lethal warehouse outlet.

But it was a foregone conclusion that the Libyans would walk away with the prize package. They had the bucks and their fearless leader, Daffy Qaddafi, had a pet project in mind. The Proteus Chain would be poured down the hated throats of the Americans like burning lye in a clogged drain.

The Mad Dog had ordered his oily emissaries to bid for it at any price. And that they had done.

The abandoned warehouse in which the Nazi cache of CBWs was stored was located in central France awaiting shipment via the heroin- and arms-smuggling corridor that stretched from the port of Marseilles through the island nation of Malta and from there to final destinations in North Africa and the Middle East.

The flow direction of contraband never varied. Arms always flowed *away* from the West. Smack and coke always flowed *toward* it.

Some problems had arisen, though. Minor ones, easily corrected. The goods should have been trucked away days before, but bad weather had prevented the freighter from docking at the port of Marseilles so that the goods could be sealifted to their ultimate stopping point, the Libyan capital city, Tripoli.

Kleist was tense as he oversaw the loading of the Nazi germ weapons onto an 18-wheel transport that would take the Proteus Chain on an overland route to the French seaport.

Maybe it was the Ghoul's Germanic instinct for punctuality. Or maybe it was the knowledge that the more time that elapsed, the higher the probability that something would go wrong. Whatever, the Nazi was as nervous as a bridegroom on a honeymoon.

The longer Kleist sat on the goods, the more the odds tilted in favor of the secret enemy that had dogged the Nazi's steps.

The Ghoul's nervousness was compounded by the powerful amphetamines he constantly swallowed. He had become addicted to methamphetamine during the war. As with many others involved in overseeing the vast network of slave-labor camps which the Third Reich had established throughout Europe, the speed had soon become an addiction for Kleist.

Kleist took two thousand milligrams of crystal meth pcr day. So dependent on it had his metabolism become that, without the speed, Kleist would lapse into a catatonic state.

This had happened once in Stockholm shortly after the war when the Ghoul's supply had dried up. He had nearly been killed then by British MI6 operatives. The Ghoul had sworn never to let it happen again. For the last thirty-five years, he had carried a suitcase filled with thousands of capsules wherever he went.

Whatever the reason for it, the waiting was making Kleist mucho edgy. He barked orders at the Nazi loading crew made up of handpicked commandos from The Spider until his grunts muttered with discontent. But each of the men bore the black-widow tattoo on their upper arm, a symbol of the elite Nazi brotherhood to which they belonged. They would continue to obey the Ghoul's orders, Kleist knew.

He would have to remember to reward them once the transaction was completed. Kleist would throw a party on the five-hundred-acre ranch he owned on the Argentinian Pampas.

There would be blonde women with large breasts in skimpy bikinis. Booze and drugs would flow. It would be like the old days in Munich when the Party was still strong, still a force that could bring a new millennium to the world.

The Ghoul's commandos were stationed all around the cavernous shell of the derelict warehouse. They were the best that The Spider had to offer.

Brave Aryan warriors, armed and trained in the latest combat techniques. The elite progeny of the SS Werewolves would defend the precious legacy of Hitler's Nazi Reich to their last drops of Aryan blood, uncontaminated by contact with inferior races, pornography, or homosexuals.

Still, they wouldn't be able to hold a candle

to a determined assault by the authorities.

And that assault would come.

Each tick of the clock, Kleist knew, brought it closer.

It was as inevitable as the rising and the setting of the sun. As inevitable as death itself.

Kleist uncapped the small vial of speed capsules and popped one into his mouth, feeling the lightning bolts flash through his nervous system as the powerful stimulant hit him like a sledgehammer chorus ringing down on the anvil of his mind.

No one inside the warehouse paid much attention to the street Gypsy stretched out on a pile of garbage in a vacant lot across from the building. Dressed in rags, the derelict rolled over every now and then before resuming his wine-soaked slumbers.

The street Gypsies were all over Europe. They beat tambourines and sold cheap trinkets and withered flowers. Mostly they begged.

If begging didn't work, they sometimes did their asking at the point of very long, very sharp knives. Not surprisingly, most people considered the Gypsies only slightly less of a nuisance than the bubonic plague, and were only too glad to ignore them at every turn.

Thirty feet above the service road which led to the warehouse from an infrequently used railroad spur, a lineman was in his cage, working on a high-tension junction box atop an electrical power pylon.

The guy had been working there since the previous day. He'd returned again that morning in his van, marked with the insignia of the power company.

Beneath the colorful logo, the hull of the van was constructed of three sandwiched layers of armored steel, capable of withstanding even a direct mortar hit. Electronic gear crowded the interior of the van.

Suspicious of the truck, Kleist had sent one of his men to call the power company from a pay phone further down the road. Zabriskie had intercepted the call inside the van, and Domino had assured the caller in perfectly accented French that the lineman was a bona fide employee of the utility.

Disguised by the company logo on the side of the van, a high-power laser gun was aimed at one of the windows of the warehouse. Invisible to the naked eye, the beam of coherent light transmitted the tiny vibrations in the pane made by sounds from inside the warehouse to digital-amplification equipment which turned it into clear, intelligible sound.

Sitting in front of the equipment console inside the van, Harry Zabriskie monitored the slowly revolving reels of tape decks as he listened in on conversations taking place within the warehouse.

The angle was bad for video surveillance, but that was compensated for by MacBeth's reports from the lineman's cage and by

Proffit, whose vantage point from his mound of garbage just across one of the warehouse's flyspecked windows allowed him to glimpse activity in the warehouse's well-lighted interior.

Z-Comm had been sitting on the warehouse for two days, surveilling the CBW transshipment point until they could determine the right moment to SLAM the goon crew and the correct tactical approach to use in setting up the target. Cage had rented a commercial helicopter at a small airport nearby and surveilled the warehouse from the air the previous day.

The strike team was operating on foreign soil on a mission that was legitimately the responsibility of the local police authorities. They were on their own hooks on strange turf.

As far as the U.S. government went, though, it was an American ball game all the way.

The Nazi germ-warfare cache stored at the warehouse for transshipment to Libya would be directed at American targets by a mad dictator sworn to attack U.S. interests every chance he got.

At the same time, there could be no United States connection should the op take a sudden nosedive.

The international repercussions would make the secret warfare that culminated in Irangate look like a bunch of schoolboys having a circle jerk.

Z-Comm gave the spooks and the politicians who paid the intelligence bills a crucial way out. The merc battalion had total deniability. If they were ever captured or killed, they would be five nonpersons.

Not Americans, not anybody.

Individuals who'd never existed.

The opposition would have a damned hard time proving that covert war against terrorism had been carried to its doorstep by a clandestine paramilitary strike force.

And even if the identities of the invisible warriors were ever made public, there was nothing concrete to tie Cage's crew to the government they served—when the duty and the pay were right.

Z-Comm would take the heat and leave the men who had sent them out into covert battlezones sitting pretty. The politicians could conduct all the Congressional hearings they wanted. In the event of failure, no heads would roll except Z-Comm's own.

Mission time was now 40 hours and counting down to the blastoff point. Z-Comm had learned a good deal during its soft probe of the warehouse, and now Cage was tasked with the job of planning the assault strategy.

The commando team had watched an assortment of vehicles entering and exiting the cul de sac on which the warehouse was situated. Photos of the men exiting the cars, faxed via satellite to the spook analysts who monitored the operation at Langely, IDd the men who came and went as bidders for the

Proteus Chain.

From Z-Comm's monitoring of conversations that had taken place inside the warehouse, Cage knew that an auction for the deadly merchandise offered by the Nazi war criminals was being held inside the derelict building.

Evidently, the quality had been judged to be acceptable, because the deal had been done and the transportation orders given. It would now be a simple matter to interdict the shipment en route to the port of Marseilles, or even once the freighter was at sea.

That wasn't the way it would go down, though.

When Z-Comm was finished, there would be no trace left of what had taken place inside the warehouse.

The Proteus Chain would be destroyed or in American hands. The warehouse would be clean and empty, a derelict building awaiting the wrecker's ball.

Cage had reached his decision.

Z-Comm would wait for the twilight of early morning to move on the target.

The team would SLAM the warehouse hard and steamroll the opposition.

Zero hour.

It was coming.

Ready or not.

NINE

Cage and Bear crouched in the predawn darkness at the front entrance of the warehouse. The large, vertically sliding panel of corrugated aluminum was pulled completely down and padlocked from the inside.

Zabriskie and Domino were already in position at the glassless frames of the casement windows a few feet above the ground level of the decaying concrete structure, while Proffit had climbed in through a window on the building's second story that gave access to a metal catwalk that ran around three sides.

He was now in position with a Colt XM177E2 Commando SMG, a shortened AR15 rifle with a telescoping butt, fitted with a Pilkington Pound sniperscope and a SIONIC silencer to back up the front and rear penetration teams as they stormed the warehouse.

Wearing combat blacksuits made of lightweight Kevlar fabric, Z-Comm prepared to SLAM-dunk the Ghoul's death depot. The team would have to neutralize the AKM-armed guard detail and lock down the lethal germ brew without exposing themselves to the highly toxic CBW agents.

The threat of the 7.62-mm tumblers that could be fired at them on sight notwithstanding, they were history if the cache of Third Reich bioweapons was damaged in any way, shape, or form. The slighest leakage of the bug cultures into the environment could easily wipe out every living thing in the ops zone.

The name of the game had to be quick in, quick out, and don't stop for any pisscalls.

The opposition might have had the numbers, but Z-Comm had the game down cold.

Cage had diagrammed the strike in the van, giving the entire operation six minutes from start to finish, no more, no less.

Z-Comm had to be surgically precise in staging the raid. Team One would blow the front door with antiarmor weapons strikes.

When they had punched a corridor into the warehouse's interior, stun grenades would be lobbed in to soften up the target for the kill.

Coming in at the rear, Team Two would blitz the strike zone as soon as they heard the HEAT blasts shatter the warehouse's front door.

They would take out any of the badguys heading for the rear exitway while Cage and Bear went in the front.

Zabriskie and Domino would hustle inside and secure the area while Proffit moved quickly through the interior of the warehouse, planting C-4 plastic packs that would be remote-detonated as the strike team sped away in the crew van.

Fast, simple, and destructive.

There was no way to fuck around with the kind of germ juice stored in the depot.

Z-Comm would obliterate the Nazi CBW agents in an incinerating inferno.

The warehouse would go up in a roiling fireball that would flash-fry whatever deadly bugs the cache contained.

"Let's get it on," Cage said to Bear. The big merc had already set up the Mk19 automatic grenade-launcher. On its standard infantry tripod mount, the Mk19 resembled a giant steel mosquito all set to deliver a painful bite.

Originally developed during the Vietnam War to equip river patrol boats operating on the Mekong Delta, the full-auto blitzer was capable of ejecting its standard magazine of 50 40-mm HE or FRAG rounds at a cycling rate of 375 rounds per minute. Its firepower was nothing short of devastating.

Squatting behind the Mk19, MacBeth set

the calibrated ladder sight for 300 meters and pointed the compensator-equipped muzzle at the center of the door. Bear took hold of the Mk19's spade grips and fired the full-auto meatgrinder.

KUH-KUH-KUH-BLAMMMMMM!

The roll-down door of corrugated sheet steel disintegrated like brittle plastic under the devastating impact of the full-auto barrage of hundreds of high-explosive mortar rounds.

Scorching tongues of flame geysered from within the noxious clouds of black smoke billowing from the huge, ragged breach in the warehouse front, licking at the two mercs as though a dragon inside had been shaken from some centuries-old sleep and now struck back in wounded rage.

Grabbing two thunderflash grenades from his chest bandolier, Cage pulled the pins on the round black balls and prepared to toss them into the smoke-filled interior. The stun grenades would simulate the optical and acoustical effects of rifle and machine-gun fire. The opposition would think they were being stormed by a platoon of soldiers instead of only two men.

The word for that was force multiplication.

Both he and MacBeth pulled down the specially treated goggles that would protect their eyes from the multiple phosphorous flashes that would disorient anybody inside. Ear plugs would muffle the sharp reports of the "flashbangs" that would add to the disorientation of the targets caught in the killzone.

As Cage and Bear hustled in through the blown warehouse entrance door, Zabriskie and Domino sprinted in the back way, their Heckler-Koch MP5A3 SMGs already in position to unleash murderous autofire at the scum nest's Nazi denizens.

As expected, a crew of well-armed Spider troopers in camo fatigues was making a fast beeline for the rear of the warehouse to escape what they believed to be a take-no-prisoners raid by a commando assault force with an overwhelming numerical superiority.

What else would they expect to come up against the stronghold—a five-man merc crew? No way, Jose.

The shooters were armed with 7.62-mm AKMs, and as soon as they saw the two black-suited figures at the warehouse rear, whipped the full-auto blasters to navel height and began throwing lead in a blind panic.

The Z-Commandos' HKs spoke first, scoring takedown after takedown in quick succession. Here a merc, there a merc, everywhere a dead merc as the 9-mm hollowpoints slammed their targets with lethal accuracy. From above, Proffit's Commando loosed deadly 5.56-x-45-mm sniper fire that scored hit after bloody hit in the combat crucible below.

The end result of the brief but sanguine encounter was to place the death depot in Z-Comm's hands in a matter of minutes.

Those Fourth Reich flunkies not mowed down in the first few seconds of the strike threw down their weapons and surrendered en masse.

Cage and Bear made them lie at gunpoint on the fractured concrete deck of the warehouse while Zabriskie and Domino frisked them for hidden weapons.

At his perch on the catwalk above, Proffit slung the Colt Commando over his shoulder and got set to unship the C-4 demolition charges from the bulging musette bags that hung from his shoulders.

Z-Comm had executed the op in just over four minutes. Well within Cage's acceptable performance parameters.

If Gunther had not been at his customary task of relieving his chronically weak bladder in a secluded corner of the warehouse, he might not have escaped Z-Comm's lightning strike.

The blacksuited strikers hadn't spotted him, though. This, Gunther knew, was his golden opportunity. The fat man would no longer be the butt of the other men's taunts. They would now be forced to respect him, to afford him all the respect he deserved.

The scumtrooper also knew that he'd be

handsomely rewarded by The Spider if he could be responsible for capturing or killing the blacksuited merc invaders.

The woman commando was the closest of the raiding party to Gunther's position. Keeping close to the concrete wall, he crept up behind the woman as silently as he could. Her back was turned toward him, making her an easy target. All it would take would be a burst of his AKM to the center of her unprotected rear to finish her off.

Then Gunther received a sudden flash of inspiration. He noticed at the last second that the woman warrior was standing beneath a heavy block and tackle. Why kill her when he could knock her unconscious? His superiors would surely want to interrogate all of the commandos.

Gunther would leave it to others to do the killing. This was not because he was squeamish, he assured himself. Despite what the other men said about him, Gunther was as willing to kill in combat as the next man.

Once he stopped retching, that is.

Gunther slung his AKM over his shoulder and released the lever on the winch control box on the wall beside him. The heavy block and tackle fell and struck Domino on the shoulder. The glancing blow was enough to deck the lady merc. Gunter had his AKM trained on her prostrate form a second later.

"The girl gets a bullet if you do not throw down your weapons," he shouted in broken

English laced with the accent of his native Argentina. "Do this now! Do not think I will fail to shoot if you disobey my order."

Z-Comm had zero options. The clown's hands were shaking, sure, but the geek had already gained the advantage. The Soviet blaster in his fists made all the difference in the world. However much of a nerd the dude was, even he couldn't miss at point-blank range.

With Domino a trigger-squeeze from death, Cage nodded to the rest of the team.

Z-Comm's weapons clattered to the fissured concrete, sounding the hollow knell of surrender.

The dozen stormtroopers who'd been sucking pavement were instantly on their combat-booted feet, retrieving automatic weapons that had been thrown in a pile after their capture.

At a command from a big bald trooper, a couple of Nazis climbed into the mammoth rig against the warehouse wall and started the powerful engine. The odor of diesel exhaust filled the musty interior of the warehouse.

Z-Comm was herded into a corner of the immense depot and placed under armed guard until it could be decided what to do with them.

Cage and his crew watched helplessly as the loaded truck was driven out of the warehouse.

They heard the roar of its powerful diesel engine fade to a dull drone as the highballing 18-wheeler disappeared down the deserted road.

TEN

From his vantage point in one of the tall trees in the pine forest surrounding the warehouse, Sam Proffit watched as a search detail from the Nazi stronghold went over Z-Comm's mobile surveillance van with a fine-toothed comb.

Sonofabitch, he cussed in a whisper.

When the demolition blitz had boomeranged on Z-Comm, Proffit had hustled out of the casement behind him, rappeled down the side of the warehouse, and doubled back to the van, where he'd hoped to retrieve some heavier armament for a bustout try.

But now that possibility had evaporated faster than ratpiss on a hot rock.

All Proffit had in the way of arms was the silenced, short-barreled Colt Commando

SMG and a few hundred rounds of the 5.56-mm ammo in web pouches on his belt. There were a couple of FRAG and APERS grenades too, hanging from ringed tabs on his blacksuit.

That wouldn't be nearly enough firepower to take care of the scum brigade inside the warehouse.

The 5.56-mm Colt was a versatile and formidable assault weapon. But it wouldn't deliver anything like the knockout punch he needed to depend on for a one-man commando assault on the Nazi hardbase.

What the job called for was the 7.62-x-51-mm steel jackets fired by the M60A1 Squad Auto Weapon in the van's weapon rack.

Getting past the grunt crew that was methodically combing through Z-Comm's mobile surveillance center was guaranteed to attract attention, though.

AKM-armed skirmishers were fanning out across the countryside looking for the escaped commando. So far he'd been able to slip through their net, but even the man someone called "the Ghost" knew he would have to move soon or run the risk of capture.

By now the warehouse crew had radioed for reinforcements, and in only a few hours Cage, Bear, Domino, and Zabriskie would be dogfood.

And every minute took the big rig with its deadly CBW cargo nearer to its final destination: Terrorist Central in Daffy Qaddafi's Libya.

Proffit decided he didn't have any choice. He'd have to push the envelope. Get the weapons from the van. Get his pards out of the warehouse.

Or get dead.

"What you did was very foolish," the cueball-domed Nazi intoned with unconcealed menace in his gravel voice. "It very nearly got us all killed."

The guy was the ranking scumtrooper in the depot. A Mauser 9-mm machine pistol was strapped across his barrel chest in a pit holster.

His right hand terminated in a stainless-steel prosthesis that was comprised of two needle-sharp hooks. One eye was a jellylike mass, slashed diagonally by a wide, puckered scar. Not only wouldn't he win any beauty contests, but the dude's breath could drop a charging rhino at 50 paces.

Cage made the hardguy as a former SS Werewolf. He appeared to be just the right age to have been part of the elite unit of behind-the-lines havockers formed by Hitler's top enforcer, Otto Skorzeny, at the end of WW II.

The elite unit of commando-trained paramilitary troops had been composed mostly of kids. Hitler Youth and old men had been all that was left of the once unstoppable Nazi

Wuehrmacht by that point in the war's paroxysmic final months. In time, these fledgling goosesteppers had become the savage nucleus of a paramilitary force based in Latin America via the CIA-Nazi "ratline."

The last dinosaurs of Hitler's Aryan superforce, these survivors of the Third Reich had trained the secret-police apparatus of more than one Third World dictatorship, including Muammar Qaddafi's in Libya.

They were protected by an intricate web of interlocking relationships that had existed long before Hitler had come to power—the treacherous web of *Die Spinne*, the Nazi Spider. Himmler's SS had been recruited from the ranks of the rich and the powerful. Strong economic ties on a global scale had never been broken. These ties had continued into the postwar period. Right up to the present day.

"You are Americans, yes?" the Hook asked. Receiving no reply, he went on, "I think a time will come soon when you will speak to me."

" 'You have ways,' is that the line?" Zabriskie told the Kraut Kojak.

The Hook's bloodless lips twitched in a Nazi's idea of a smile and he took a deep drag on his cigar.

"You Americans. You think we were all stereotypes like Conrad Veidt in *Casablanca*. A race of psychopaths and perverts. But in reality it was those who fought against us that were mad. What we offered the world was far better than the legacy you have been left with.

"Degenerates and scum have inherited the postwar world. Your society is infected with AIDS. Drug addicts and homosexuals have robbed you of your self-respect. The streets of your cities belong to pimps, thieves, and murderers. We offered the gift of order and you spat in our faces. In the world we would have forged with blood and steel none of these degenerates would exist, except in the grave."

Stubbing out the cigar, the Hook continued, "But we do have our 'ways,' *jah*, my American friend. The same methods you yourselves employ. In a little while a physician we use in Lyon will arrive. The doctor is skilled in the use of chemicals.

"Under the chemicals you will tell us what we want to know, rest assured. But the chemicals are a sword which cuts both ways. You may all end up as vegetables. Tell us who you are and what you wanted here. It doesn't matter. In the end it's all a game anyway."

"Tell me something," MacBeth asked the Hook with a serious look on his face. "You got a hook on the end of your prick too?"

The Nazi's face went ashen.

A muscle pulsed spasmodically beneath his mutilated right eye, making the ugly scar twitch obscenely.

With surprising speed and agility for a

man his size, the Hook whipped the Mauser from its chest holster and jammed the SS autopistol into MacBeth's midsection.

His entire body began to tremble violently. He was a big fucker, almost as tall as MacBeth was. The Hook glared eye to eye with the Bear.

"Swinefucking dog," he said in a voice that was a razor-edge whisper. "I could kill you now. But I promise you that what awaits you will be far worse than any bullet. I will make certain that the doctor gives you a special needle. One which will make you grovel at the tips of my boots. In the end you will beg for the bullet that will end your life."

"Damn!" MacBeth returned deadpanned. "I thought we were gonna play poker next Friday night!"

The hook turned to the AKM-wielding hardmen who bracketed him.

"Richter! Keitel!" he barked. "Guard these tin soldiers. If they move, shoot to kill." To Bear he said. "I will enjoy watching you grovel."

Spitting on the floor, the big man holstered the Mauser, turned his back on Z-Comm, and stalked off, his combat boots beating out a loud tattoo on the shattered concrete of the Nazi strongbase.

The silenced Commando SMG wheezed twice. The sound of the closely spaced 5.56-mm autobursts was completely masked by the background noise of traffic on the highway that was a few hundred yards from the warehouse, but completely obscured from it by heavily forested terrain.

A crimson geyser shot from the pulped skull of the goon guy nearest Proffit's position as a three-round butterfly of 5.56-mm hollowpoints burst his head as though it were a ketchup-filled balloon.

Minus its noggin, the corpse sagged to its knees and crashed forward, watering the grass with its blood.

Brittt! Britt! Burrrrritttt!

Proffit triggered another 5.56-mm death-burst at the second camo-fatigued trooper posted to guard the van just as he spun to face him. Reflexes jerked the AKM he toted to hip level.

But the creep's reaction time was nowhere fast enough to save his skin. Proffit's next Commando autoburst slammed him in the belly, shearing away intestines, stomach wall, liver, and spleen and catapulting him backward with arms and legs outstretched comically in death.

Proffit was across the few yards of open ground and inside the scout van in seconds.

Time slowed to an eternity measured in pulsebeats as Proffit grabbed the gear he needed before an assault from the depot had a chance to materialize.

A couple of seconds were all he needed, though.

Proffit unracked the M60 manstopper and loaded up with hundreds of rounds of belted

7.62-mm ammo. He also grabbed blocks of C-4 plastic and miniature electronic timers, plus as many grenades as he could cram into a large canvas rucksack.

NATO-caliber studs kicked up dust and whined off chrome as Proffit exited the van. A lightning head-turn confirmed the five-man hit brigade hustling toward the van with guns blazing.

Crouching a few yards from the crew van, Proffit swung the big M60 SAW to face the commando heat and returned a longburst of blitzing 7.62s.

The fast-cycling steeljackets killed two AKM gunners instantly. They went down fast, like marionettes with cut guy-wires, forcing the rest of the crew to dive helter-skelter for cover.

Reinforcements were coming up fast, though. Too fast and with too many numbers for Proffit to risk holding his position. Temporarily dropping the SAW, he pulled FRAG grenades from the webbing at his chest and pitched the black deathballs toward the line of fire.

Multiple explosions burped up a cloud of dust and tremored the ground as Proffit hustled on a low crouch into the cover of the forestland surrounding the warehouse.

As he disappeared into the woods beyond the strike zone, Proffit could hear the commotion of many confused and frightened men shouting a disarray of conflicting orders.

The Z-Commando smiled grimly.

He always did when things were starting to get real.

ELEVEN

It had been a long, hot drive from the doctor's office in Lyon to the warehouse in the hills of the Haute-Loire district. The medico was not in the best of moods. It was late on a drizzly Sunday morning, and the call had awakened him from a hung-over sleep.

But the people who had placed the call were not the sort one told to call back during business hours. So the doctor had held his tongue, filled his black leather satchel with the implements of his trade, and awaited the black SEL that was to take him on the long road journey.

"The woman first," he now said, rolling up his shirtsleeves. As two camo-suited gorillas held Domino down, he pulled open her eyelids and shone a light into her eyes. Nodding, he clicked off the penlight and took Domino's blood pressure. "Yes, I think she will make an excellent subject," he said when his examination had been completed.

Behind the thick lenses of his aviator-style glasses, the doctor's eyes gleamed with reptilian hate. He did not like women. Beautiful ones especially.

The drugs he had brought with him would make her writhe in convulsions of exquisite agony as they caused irreparable damage to the motor and speech centers of the brain as well as almost complete memory loss. He would enjoy watching the woman transformed into a drooling imbecile within minutes of receiving the injection.

His penis was already erect as he contemplated the sight of her body on the hard ground in the grotesque throes of lacerating pain. Perhaps they would even let him have her when they were finished, as they sometimes had done before. The doctor would have to remember to ask. Certainly a good job on his part would be an inducement to his employers to accede to his wishes.

"Hold her," the doctor ordered the Nazi knuckle-draggers. Each merc grabbed one arm and pinned Domino down. "This will not take long," the doctor said calmly as he plunged a hypodermic needle into a vial of clear liquid and began to slowly fill the syringe.

"In the beginning, she may go into violent

convulsions, but these will last only a few seconds. She may also vomit and void her bladder and bowels. Hold her tightly, understand? Under no circumstances are you to let go of her."

The guards nodded and braced themselves. The doctor wrenched the hypo from the bottle with an ugly squeak and squirted a few drops into the air to test the syringe.

"So, young lady . . ." he said huskily as he brought the needle close to Domino's bare arm. "Now we will, as you Americans say, get it on."

Springing up from a low crouch, Proffit took out an AKM-toting Spider man outside the front of the warehouse with a quick stab of his K-BAR combat knife into the soft spot behind the left ear that instantly destroyed the brain stem.

As the guard went limp as overcooked pasta, Proffit caught him around the middle and dragged the body into the high grass where it would be hidden from view.

He had seen the Mercedes SEL pull up in front and the man with the black medical bag exit with a crew of windbreaker-jacketed hardguys. Proffit had a good idea of what was happening inside and knew that he had to move quickly. When they called in the Sister Morphines they were getting desperate.

Proffit removed a four-ounce brick of C-4 and molded the puttylike high explosive to form a spiral on the side of the warehouse. He next pressed a radio-triggered remote detonator into the C-4 and flipped on the arming switch. The shaped plastic charge wasn't the greatest work of art Proffit had ever sculpted, but he knew the punks inside would get a real bang out of it.

At a button-press, the charge would blow a 20-foot hole in the side of the building.

Proffit hauled ass to the opposite end of the warehouse and hunkered down behind a mound of garbage, feeling his heart jackhammer in his chest.

His breathing deepened as his veins filled with adrenaline and his brain took on a sharp, sudden clarity that was the mark of combat exhilaration.

That exhilarataion could never be explained to anybody who had never experienced it for himself. It was a primitive emotion, triggered by the nearness of death and as ancient and as powerful as mankind's cellular need for violent combat.

Snapping a 30-round clip of 5.56-mm rounds into his Commando assault weapon, Proffit studded it to fire three-round bursts and slung the Colt SMG over his shoulder. He hooked the box mag of 100 7.62-x-51 meat-eaters onto the side of the M60A1 SAW and snapped the distintegrating link belt into the Squad Auto's receiver.

Taking a deep breath, he punched the black central button on the remote radio detonator.

KUHHHH-THOOOOOMMMMM!

Proffit waited two beats, giving the badasses inside time to turn en masse toward the diversionary blast, and went in duckwalk fashion, hosing down the warehouse interior with M60 assault fire.

The diversion worked beautifully. Proffit caught the Nazi merc crew lined up like clay pigeons in the direction of the blast. His first longburst swept the interior with withering fire that mowed down the stunned men inside like stalks of wheat before the reaper's scythe.

With his free hand, Proffit pulled an APERS grenade from chest webbing and pitched the lethal black stingball.

Whump!

Violent concussion rings picked up bodies and flung them into the air while jagged steel splinters made mincemeat out of internal organs.

The first grenade toss was followed by another and still another as the M60 SAW kept up a staccato accompaniment to the deep basso of the APERS strikes.

Nobody applauded. They were too busy turning belly-up.

Proffit could see the Z-Commandos at the other end of the cavernous interior of the depot. Keeping up a steady, pounding rhythm of 7.62-mm suppression fire that forced the opposition to keep their heads down, the man they called "the Ghost" punched a crimson corridor through to their position.

Z-Comm had been waiting for Proffit to come in after them. When the two AKM-armed goons had turned toward the explosion the merc crew knew that the cavalry had arrived and reacted instantly and savagely.

In that moment Cage and Zabriskie, nearest the guards, had grabbed the AKMs away from them. The fact that the guards had becn armed with rifles instead of compact automatic sidearms was a stupid tactical error that marked the Hook as an amateur, for all his swaggering bravado.

Prisoners should never be guarded by men with rifles. Long-barreled weapons are too easy to take easy.

All it takes is a sharp, sudden twist at the right moment.

Zabriskie and Cage followed up the grab maneuvers with skull-busting butt-smashes to the jaw and head of each trooper, knocking them senseless to the concrete.

They were blasting away with a 7.62-mm steelstorm before the unconscious men even hit the ground.

The interior of the warehouse was now gripped by the chaos of a full-auto firestorm, as hot as the blazing center of Perdition.

Zabriskie and Bear had their own priorities. Zabriskie dodged flying 7.62 studs as he climbed up a steel ladder to the upper level and the former office room where Doctor Feelbad was working on Domino.

Shooting off the door lock and kicking it in, he saw the doctor with the needle poised a hairsbreadth from the woman warrior's forearm.

The two gorillas pinning Domino to the floor let go of her and frantically struggled to bring their weapons into play. A longburst of 7.62 tumblers blew them away like straw dogs in a scorching whirlwind.

Domino was now tussling with the drug doctor. She had his bony hand in a wristlock as he struggled to plunge the needle into the vein in her arm.

Zabriskie smashed the AKM's buttstock across the back of the doctor's head.

He sagged sideways, whirling around as he crashed backwards into the wall with the hypodermic needle embedded in his pulsating throat. Almost instantly the doctor began going into convulsive seizures. His arms and legs thrashed uncontrollably and a bloody foam sudsed from his mouth as he bit off his tongue and chewed it to a red, frothing pulp.

Zabriskie finished off the doc with a mercy burst, and he and Domino hustled from the room as the lady merc scooped up one of the downed guards' AKMs.

In the meltdown below, Frank MacBeth and the Hook were getting it on, one-on-one. The humongous Nazi hardman swung at the merc man-mountain with an arm the size of a treetrunk.

The glittering prosthesis on its end whistled as it cleaved the air. Bear ducked and lashed out with a savage thrust kick that slammed the Nazi in his midsection, knocking the wind out of him as he violently lurched sideways.

MacBeth closed in, but the Nazi kicked upward with both feet, delivering a crushing double-smash to the gut that staggered the Bear.

The Hook regained his footing and swung the razor-sharp steel prosthesis in a glittering arc aimed at MacBeth's face. Bear sidestepped the death swing, but just barely.

After gouging two bloody stripes in MacBeth's cheek, the steel hooks became embedded in the crumbling masonry of the building's wall. Bear pulled a K-BAR from his boot scabbard on the follow-through and swung with all his might, feeling the shock of contact all the way up to his shoulder socket.

The tempered steel blade of the K-BAR hacked off the Hook's artificial hand. The former Werewolf howled in demented agony as the glittering prosthesis slid across the cement floor of the warehouse like some enormous cockroach skittering for cover.

Blood jetted in black gouts from the end of Hook's arm stump like black water from a ruptured sewage pipe. MacBeth kicked the big merc and he went flying into the wall, impaling himself on rusted spikes that projected from the water-stained concrete surface. The Bear's last sight of the Nazi was as he struggled to pull his body free of the rusty cross to which he was nailed.

"Looks like you passed the multiple-choice but failed the essay," MacBeth told the struggling Nazi. "Better luck next lifetime, amigo."

Zabriskie and Domino linked up with Proffit and Cage in mopping up the remaining opposition, most of whom had already lost their appetite for combat and were now fleeing the scene of carnage in droves.

Hustling across the corpse-strewn floor, Z-Comm broke for the fields surrounding the warehouse.

At the blown entrance, they paused while Proffit pitched a satchel charge containing a time-fused C-4 brick into the warehouse.

The fierce explosion snapped off the top of the building as if it were a bottlecap and sent it rocketing skyward on a broiling pillar of fire.

The walls trembled, then vaporized as they were blown outward in an avalanche of ruptured concrete.

The flaming wreckage collapsed with a thunderclap that shook the ground as Z-Comm sprinted across the wasteland toward the commo van.

They did not see the flaming human figure that had crashed through a splintering casement window an instant before the explosion thundered through the warehouse. Nor did they see it rise shakily to its feet after the concussive force of the blast extinguished the flames that engulfed it and stumble off into the forest, beyond the burning zone of destruction.

"We will meet again," growled the Hook as he turned back toward the blast zone. "Count on it."

TWELVE

With Zabriskie at the wheel, the Mercedes SEL in which Z-Comm had sped away from the microwaved warehouse negotiated the hairpin turns of the steep mountain roads whipsawing southward toward France's Mediterranean coastline.

AKM fire had blown the crew van's tires during Proffit's raid on the mobile unit to grab the M60 SAW. In any event, the van would not have been fast or maneuverable enough for the high-performance driving needed to overtake the highballing 18-wheeler laden with Nazi bugs.

Portable commo gear salvaged from the crippled van put the sleek German sedan in touch with Cage and Proffit in a chartered helicopter hovering above the Paris-

Marseilles superhighway a few miles down the line.

By now the big rig that had busted out of the warehouse already had several hours' lead on Z-Comm. It was over three hundred miles to the southern French coast, though, and Z-Comm still stood a chance of heading off the monster semi before it reached its destination.

Even at top speed, the speedwagon would need at least another day to make the port of Marseilles. There it would be surrounded by a small army of armed thugs who controlled the lucrative express stop along the Paris-to-Istanbul smuggling pipeline.

Z-Comm had burned rubber to the airport where the chopper Cage had chartered to recce the warehouse from the air sat on its pad, and launched an air-land search for the runaway 18-wheeler. While the Mercedes followed the main highway in pursuit of the target vehicle, the chopper scanned the webwork of main and arterial routes from its skyborne vantage point.

If the truck was sighted on any of the secondary routes, then so much the better. There'd still be enough lead time to allow the Mercedes to turn off onto an arterial road and catch up with the speeding semi. Also, a less heavily traveled road would provide Z-Comm with the most shooter-friendly set of circumstances for an ambush.

An average two-laner that switchbacked

between stands of trees without much traffic would give Z-Comm the opportunity to set up a workable roadblock, as well as providing cover and sufficient time for a getaway before other motorists happened along.

A little outside the small industrial town of Montelimar in the Rhone Valley, the portable commo unit—an AN/PRC 112 tactical radio—MacBeth carried squawked with an incoming transmission from Cage in the chopper a few klicks to the south.

"Rodan to Big Bad Wolf," Cage's voice crackled over the air-land comlink. "We've sighted Little Red Riding Hood."

In the Bell AT63's cockpit, Cage and Proffit looked down on the narrow blacktop ribbon that snaked through the craggy mountain country, switchbacking down toward the topaz waters of the Mediterranean. The secondary route paralleled the rocky French coastline, which was separated from the road by forested hill country.

Maybe the truck's wheelman had been motivated to turn off the Paris-Marseilles superhighway in an attempt to shake off the possibility of pursuit. And maybe he was just too spooked to think straight.

Whatever his reasons, the turn of events was favorable to Z-Comm. The road was almost free of traffic. Its twists and turns between tree-lined stretches made it the ideal place to stage a roadblock. Z-Comm could stop the truck, incapacitate its crew, incinerate the rig with C-4 charges, and be out of the strike zone in minutes.

"Big Bad Wolf to Rodan," MacBeth said back into the mike as he kept his eyes on the road ahead. "Report your position."

Cage gave Bear the chopper's position and a general description of the terrain below. MacBeth checked these particulars against the roadmap that lay flat on the seat between himself and Zabriskie, while Domino leaned over the front seat and followed the back-and-forth.

"I copy that," Bear said back after a few beats. "There's a turnoff about a quarter of a mile up the line. With a little luck I figure we can catch up with Little Red Riding Hood in around twenty minutes."

"Roger that," Cage returned. "Will advise of any changes. Out."

The next turnoff was coming up fast and Zabriskie was in the four-lane highway's leftmost lane with a big truck pacing the fast-moving Mercedes in the next lane over to the right. Hanging out the window, MacBeth signaled for a turn but the driver didn't want to hear anything about it, flipping Bear the bird in response.

"Hold onto your assholes," Zabriskie hollered, stomping the gas pedal and wrenching the steering wheel full around to send the Mercedes into a fishtailing skid that catapulted it only a few inches ahead of the big rig's front end before the Mercedes cleared the lane.

The truck's driver leaned on the semi's diesel horn and shot the Mercedes a couple of hand signals understandable only to Sicilians as it zoomed past his rig.

The SEL's tires screamed as the car dry-planed into the shoulder a little ahead of the turnoff. Another wrench of the wheel and the Mercedes was accelerating around the U-shaped curve into the secondary road Cage had reported the truck's position on.

Just short of 30 minutes later, the SEL pursuit crew had established visual contact with the truck they were chasing.

The big 18-wheeler was just a couple of car-lengths up the road, which zigzagged dizzily between stretches of deciduous forest on either side. Zabriskie slowed the SEL until they were five car-lengths behind the cargo rig.

Domino and Bear checked their weapons in preparation for the capture of the truck, mindful of several potential problems that the operation would present.

For example, they weren't certain how many Spider mercs from the warehouse had gotten away from the shootout on board the truck. But they had to count on finding a well-armed crew that was on the alert for trouble. The bad dudes would have to be expecting some attempt to be made to blitz them before they reached their destination.

"Big Bad Wolf to Rodan," Bear said into the slim olive drab radio link to Cage and Proffit in the helo above them. "We're right behind Red Riding Hood. It's wheel-of-fortune time. Over."

Cage swung the light, maneuverable helo in a wide arc that swept it low over the stretch of pine forest on the mountainside between the road and the ocean and brought it a few hundred yards ahead of the truck.

Two miles up the road, Cage noted, the blacktop zigzagged sharply to one side, then dipped between two wooded stretches before it leveled off to a straightaway that ran for a couple miles more.

Cage judged the upcoming road-bend the perfect place to stop the truck with a two-flank ambush. The semi would be forced to idle down into low gear as it cornered the tricky dogleg in the road. The driver would be concentrating on taking the turn, not on what was happening in the air and on the roadbed's perimeter.

"Big Bad Wolf," Cage said into the comset. "Cut ahead of Red Riding Hood. There's a bend about a mile ahead. Block the road. Over."

"Roger that, Rodan," Bear said back. "Out."

Nodding, Zabriskie upshifted from third to fifth and simultaneously put the SEL's pedal to the metal.

The superbly crafted overhead cam engine growled like some lithe jungle cat springing into action as it went from 30 to 90 MPH in just under three seconds, catapulting the car down the center of the broken white line until it was almost bumper to bumper with the big rig that took up most of the straightaway.

Zabriskie leaned on the horn and the speedwagon jogged reluctantly to the right to allow the small passenger vehicle to shoot up the road on its passing side.

As the the SEL crew shot ahead of the truck's cab, MacBeth flashed his best Colgate smile at the driver. The guy had a thick mustache, close-cropped hair, and jaws clamped so tightly the cheek muscles jerked with tension.

He didn't return Bear's cheerful howdy-do. His black eyes glittered in his pallid white face with cold menace.

MacBeth could see another dude in the cab's shotgun seat, but could not guess at how many other cruds might be inside the cargo area or what kind of artillery the shitbags would be packing. It was an even bet, though, that both guys up front were packing AKM autorifles and probably automatic sidearms too.

With the speedometer redlined near 110 MPH, Zabriskie continued rocketing the Mercedes up the straightaway until it had left the slower truck a solid half mile behind it.

Hollering for Bear and Domino to hold on, Zabriskie stomped on the parking brake while simultaneously flooring the pedal and pulled a Hollywood-perfect bootleg turn that spun the Mercedes in a 180-degree arc in less than a second so that it stopped diagonally across the narrow roadway.

The three Z-Commandos hustled from the SEL and took up positions in the deep, grass-lined drainage ditches on either side of the road. Weapons at the ready, they waited for the truck to materialize from out of the dazzling heat shimmer.

Seconds later, they heard the grinding of gears as the truck's driver downshifted in preparation for the hairpin turn.

The cab of the big rig came out of the heat shimmer like the head of some time-warped prehistoric monster as it passed around the curving road a pulsebeat later.

MacBeth fired a warning burst from the M60 he fisted in each black-gloved hand, sending chunks of macadam flying up into the truck's grillwork.

Initially, the semi slowed, but then the strike team could see the guy in the shotgun seat put a gun to the wheelman's head and jerk his hand forward.

You didn't have to read sign language to know what he was telling him.

The driver poured on the gas and plowed into the Mercedes that was blocking its path across the narrow road.

With a stomach-turning crunch, the truck bulldozed the Mercedes aside like an elephant tusking away a small, agile predator. From their positions in the ditches on either side of the road, the Z-Commandos poured autofire at the truck as it roared past, but it was already too late to score a direct hit on the men in the cab.

"Damn!" Cage yelled to Proffit in the chopper overhead. "They didn't go for it."

The truck was already several hundred yards in front of the damaged Mercedes. Zabriskie climbed behind the dented vehicle's wheel and miraculously got the engine to turn over. Bear and Domino piled into the expensive German wreckage and they took off after the fleeing rig.

Suddenly the back doors of the truck flew open and the snouts of automatic weapons appeared.

Zabriskie had just enough time to violently swerve the Mercedes to one side as a LAW warhead sped toward them and detonated a few feet from the car's rear fender.

A couple of inches closer and shrapnel would have ruptured the fuel tank and blown the SEL and its occupants to kindgom come.

Cage swooped the helo down on the truck. There would be no chance now to ambush the vehicle. It would have to be kayoed permanently.

Proffit readied the Colt Commando. It already had the bulb-ended Mecar 40-mm HEAT round projecting from its muzzle. Banking steeply, Cage made a low, arcing pass across the cab of the speedballing semi, and Proffit sighted the Commando's trough sight on the front of the truck's cargo area.

Angling the Colt through the open hatch of the chopper's plexiglass bubble dome, Proffit sighted on the road surface in front of the cab.

A trigger pull launched the HEAT round, which detonated with a loud *Crump!* and a geyser of dirt a few feet ahead of the truck's front end.

The driver swerved violently as the high-explosive anti-tank round's shuddering impact lifted the front wheels off the black-top for a heartbeat and almost lost control of the wheel.

The big truck's tires wailed like banshees as it skidded off the blacktop, spinning without purchase in the drainage ditches and kicking up clouds of brown road dust.

But still the wheelman wouldn't stop the rig. Either he was plain panicked or the gun-waver in the seat beside him was a bigger and more immediate threat than the airborne shooters in the darting and weaving dragonfly overhead.

Whatever his reasons, he continued high-balling the rig around the tortuously twisting mountain road. The truck lurched from side to side like some wounded prehistoric behemoth trying desperately to outrun a pack of meat-eating predators.

Cage banked the helo for another bombing run as one of the shooters punched up through a hatch on the top of the truck and poured withering firepower from an AKM at the helo that buzzed overhead like an angry hornet.

A red line of glowing tracer slugs tore

through the AT43's plexiglass dome, missing Cage and Proffit by a hairsbreadth as the chopper swooped out of the line of 7.62-mm fire.

As Cage brought the chopper into position for another 40-mm mortar strike, Proffit sighted on the side of the truck and squeezed the Commando's trigger.

An instant later, a gaping rupture appeared in the truck's hull, followed by billowing clouds of voluminous black smoke. The machine gunner had disappeared back into the inferno inside the cargo area.

The lethal steel dragonfly buzzed the big rig again, its skids almost touching its smoke-belching roof.

This time autofire erupted from the SMG clutched in the hands of the hardguy in the passenger seat of the semi's cab.

The line of 9-x-19-mm slugs went wide of the fast-darting chopper, though, and Proffit was able to put another Mecar HEAT round only a foot from the semi's right front wheel.

The mammoth rig lurched drunkenly as one of its bigfoot tires suddenly exploded and flew off the spinning metal rim.

In the cab, the driver fought the wheel to regain control of the careening semi. But the truck was behaving even more violently now, its cargo area in flames, leaving behind a trail of voluminous dark smoke as it fishtailed on the treacherous road surface.

"Why the hell doesn't he stop?" Cage asked Proffit above the roar of the rotors. "The rig's crippled."

"Maybe he can't," Proffit offered.

Whatever the reason, the rig was coming up on a hairpin turn that would have been impossible to negotiate in a vehicle its size without slowing to grade gear.

At the speed it was traveling, though, there was no way in hell it would be able to slow in time to safely negotiate the treacherous turn.

Cage and Proffit watched helplessly from the air as the truck's cab crashed through the flimsy aluminum barrier at the perimeter of the road and plunged headlong over the edge of the highway into the wooded slopes of the mountainside.

The cargo hold of the truck went next, breaking away from the cab as the two sections of the rig tumbled end-over-end into the deep gorge below, where they struck with sickening crashes and burst into flames in a series of multiple explosions.

Hovering over the crash zone in the chopper, Cage and Proffit could see the flaming wreckage strewn all over the bottom of the gorge, where the flames soon spread to the surrounding timber.

The battered Mercedes pulled over at the roadside where a line of smoking rubber skidmarks marked the place where the truck had gone over.

"One thing's for sure," Cage said to Proffit as he banked the chopper steeply to set it down near the rest of the strike team.

"Whatever was onboard that truck, it wasn't the cache of Nazi biologicals."

"Why's that?" asked Proffit.

"Because if that had been the case," replied Cage, "there would have been enough deadly germ agents released on impact to kill Bear, Zabriskie, and Domino by now."

Cage set the chopper down a few yards from the strike team and picked up Zabriskie, Domino, and Bear.

He banked the helo steeply on a flight path toward the airfield.

Cage's suspicions were confirmed by the police and agents of the DST, the French Security Service, on inspection of the wreck.

There was no evidence of anything onboard in the nature of CBW weapons.

All that had been pulled from the flaming debris of the wreckage were the remains of extensive files of war-era Nazi weapons-development projects and charred fragments of metal that could not be identified initially but which were believed to have been part of an as-yet-unknown secret weapon of the Third Reich.

While all of this was of interest to the intelligence boys, what mattered most to Z-Comm was that Kleist's deadly bugs had not been on board the truck. This pointed to a single inescapable conclusion.

They had already reached Libya.

The hoard of Nazi germ warfare agents was now certainly in the possession of Colonel Muammar Qaddafi, the Mad Dog of the Middle East.

BOOK TWO:

Reach Out and Snuff Someone

THIRTEEN

Juddering to a halt, the Libyan Arab Airlines DC9 Airbus from Jedeida Airport near Tunis, Tunisia, completed a successful landing at Tripoli International Airport a few miles outside of Tripoli, Libya.

The shuttle flight had taken approximately one hour from point of departure to point of arrival.

As soon as the small commercial jetliner began taxiing toward the terminal's boarding gate, the passengers unbuckled and began surging toward the plane's forward hatchway in a display of bad manners that seemed to be a univeral constant among air travelers, transcending all differences of culture and national origin.

Half of the plane seemed to contain Arab

businessmen, the other half Italians.

This was not surprising.

The Italians' relationship with Libya was much the same as the U.S. relationship with Mexico and Latin America. Like Morocco, it was a source of plentiful raw materials and dirt-cheap labor. Whether you called these relationships imperialistic or not, there was always a joker in the deck.

For the spaghetti-benders, it meant their tough stand on terrorism at home would always be vulnerable to a commercial ally that was one of terrorism's chief sponsors. For America, it had meant supporting the corrupt regimes of Central American heroin honchos whose main business involved putting junk into the needles that went into American veins and who ran their banana republics practically as sidelines.

Cage and Domino waited for the aisle to clear before cracking open the overhead storage bins and pulling down their carry-on luggage.

They returned the smiles of the flight attendants who watched the deplaning passengers, then walked along the overheated tarmac and into the crowded arrivals lounge, following the signs directing passengers to Libyan passport control located on the terminal's ground-floor promenade.

This lowest level of the terminal swarmed with people, most of whom were dressed in traditional Arab garb. Men and women alike wore flowing robes, the former sporting burnooses over their heads, the latter with veils that covered the lower halves of their faces. Other men wore the traditional Arab headgear with Western-style suits.

Despite the air-conditioning, the terminal was hotter than Mexican heartburn. But that was okay. It was the dry heat.

Posted throughout the terminal were commando troops in ODs and red berets wielding Italian-made PM12S submachine guns. Through the plate-glass window of the terminal, Cage noticed a Libyan Jetstar troop transport plane sitting on the runway.

It too had a military guard posted, this one shouldering a Kalashnikov autorifle and standing at attention in the baking heat. Maybe it was good for his allergies.

Passport control consisted of a couple of security desks near two slowly revolving baggage carousels. Cage and Domino waited on the shorter of the two lines and presented their U.S. passports to a Libyan customs officer in a short-sleeved khaki uniform and a peaked cap who glowered as he flipped through the pages.

Taking his time, the customs man waved over a military officer in ODs and conferred with him in rapid-fire Arabic. Finally, he looked at Cage and spat out a string of guttural sentences, waving around the passports he clutched in his hands. Cage shrugged.

"You oughta do something about that dandruff problem, guy," he told the shouting

Libyan.

"There you are. Hell, I was afraid I'd missed you." A dude was huffing and puffing after running up to Cage and Domino, while pushing his way through the crowded terminal.

He was big, had hairy arms, and talked American pretty good. His forehead was high. His face was a cement slab. Two shards of green beer-bottle glass embedded in it passed for eyes. Perspiration filmed his flat brow and formed two half-moons under the armpits of his short-sleeved epaulette shirt.

Cage had been expecting him.

The newcomer draped his beefy arm around the immigration officer's bunched shoulders and shot him some rapid-fire raghead-speak.

This seemed to have an immediate effect. The immigration man relaxed and nodded as the guy spoke to him, stealing glances at Cage and Domino between nods, his nods getting deeper and his glances getting longer the more the new guy spoke to him.

When the palaver was finished, the customs officer briskly stamped their passports and handed them back, this time with a bad try at a smile on his sweaty face.

"Don't worry about your bags," the dude in the safari shirt told Cage and Domino. "I'll have them sent over."

He pulled out a pack of Egyptian cigarets and lit one up. "Please let me apologize. We had some trouble getting out here in time.

You should have been passed right through. Heads are going to roll, believe me."

"No problem," Cage told the guy. "What was the hassle all about anyway?"

"Customs Officer Shajad doesn't like Americans, apparently," the guy responded with a short braying laugh. "He decided that it would be in the interest of Libyan national health to have both of you given full body-cavity strip searches to make sure you weren't bringing any contraband and/or AIDS viruses into the country. I assured him that if he did not stamp your passports as of five minutes ago, Colonel Qaddafi would hear of it personally and his genitals would be snipped off with rusty garden shears shortly thereafter."

An Arab driver wordlessly took their bags and deposited them in the trunk of a black Lincoln Town Car stretch limo with VIP plates parked in front of the terminal.

Cage and Domino climbed into the back seat, immediately chilled by the LC's air-conditioned interior. The guy who had met them got in the passenger seat up front. He barked commands at the native driver in Arabic and they sped away from the airport terminal.

Cage watched the desert scenery zip past on the highway leading toward Tripoli.

The face that was reflected back as a transparent overlay across the velocity-blurred desert landscape was not his own.

It had been altered by careful cosmetic

changes to hide his features. Cage now sported a Van Dyke beard that matched the color of his hair. His natural steel-gray had been dyed brown.

Contact lenses had changed the color of his eyes, and a chemical skin peel had temporarily bleached out the half-moon scar on the right side of his lean jaw.

For the duration of his stay in Libya, he would no longer be Logan Cage. The cover he would use would be that of "Lucien Cloede," an international arms broker who specialized in big-ticket weapons sales and was a master of the fine art of forged end-users certificates.

Cloede was a naturalized West German who had received American citizenship with the precise intention of doing business in the lucrative U.S.A. Cloede—the real Cloede, that is—was also currently recuperating from a heart attack at a Swiss medical clinic.

The heart attack had been induced by a few drops of sodium morphate in the morning coffee served Cloede at the ritzy ski lodge in Lugano, Italy, where he had been staying.

Lugano is only a few miles from the Swiss border. Sodium morphate is untraceable. It is also a favorite Mafia micky. The Mafia was paying some dues to the Italian intelligence bureau, SIS.

Italian agents on the hospital staff, including the doctor who was treating the wealthy arms broker, would see to it that Cloede remained heavily sedated for the duration of

Z-Comm's mission inside Libya.

The Italians were well placed to operate inside Switzerland, sharing a common northern border with the Swiss. Both the Italian SIS and its paramilitary rapid-deployment force, Forza Di Rapido Intervento, owed Cage and his commando team a debt for its help in averting a bloodbath in Venice when the Vulture's terror crews had tried to blitz the U.S.-Soviet summit meeting held there.

Returning Z-Comm's favor now would make them even.

Domino posed as Cloede's mistress, going by the handle of April Showers, amateur Vegas showgirl, professional girlfriend to the rich and famous.

With her raven-black hair dyed a platinum blonde and an outfit so tacky no self-respecting hooker would be caught dead in it, Domino had the part nailed down tight.

The beautiful female commando clutched Cage's arm as the Lincoln stretch sped along the highway, then turned off onto an exit ramp leading to the outskirts of the Libyan capital city and its chief maritime port.

"Oooh," Domino squealed with mock delight. "Is that really Tripoli I see over there? Shit, it looks like Reno!"

A city—part Arabian Nights, part urban nightmare—rose suddenly in the distance as they came toward the turn. Its tall spires and onion-domed minarets were interspersed with multi-story high-rise office buildings of poured concrete and stressed steel. The city stood against a line of jagged mountain peaks to the west, and the mouth of the Gulf of Sidra to its east.

"Yup, that's Tripoli, all right," the guy up front said. "Libya's capital city and seat of her government."

"Will we get to meet Colonel Qaddafi?" Domino asked in a Betty Boop falsetto that matched her hair and clothes perfectly and would tag her once and for all as a bubble-brained blonde. "I think he's cute enough to eat for breakfast."

"The colonel's real busy," returned their host. "But then again, you never know."

The man in the front seat laughed. These days, Qaddafi spent a lot of his time in drag and makeup.

The colonel was losing his mind. But his camel humping public considered him tantamount to some kind of god-king.

"Better watch the lady, Mr. Cloede," the guy up front told Cage with a wink. "She's too good-looking not to take seriously when she talks like that."

Cage smiled. "I always take beautiful women seriously," he said, cupping Domino's chin and looking into her eyes. "And call me Lucky. All my friends do."

"I'll be happy to . . . Lucky," the guy up front returned with a shit-eating farmboy grin that spoke eloquently of his rural Nebraska origins. "If you'll call me Miles."

"A pleasure, Miles," Cage returned. Cage

didn't add that he would consider it an even bigger pleasure to call him something else: history.

The man in the front seat was the lowest species of ratprick to Logan Cage. A man who'd sold out his country for 30 pieces of silver.

Miles O'Bannion had innocent blood on his hands. There was a terminate on sight order out on him. Well deserved too.

The ex-CIA agent had escaped a Company dragnet after he had been exposed as a triple who whored both sides of the street and did dirty deals with the scum honchos of banana-land for good measure.

But treason wasn't enough for O'Bannion. The fucker had to spit on America on top of betraying her. Through a circuitous path that involved dummy companies, O'Bannion had singlehandedly staged the biggest arms scam of the century. He had succeeded in diverting enough U.S. weaponry to Muammar Qaddafi to equip a small army.

Which is precisely what the Libyans did. The arms went into the bloodstained hands of Terrorist International.

The arms were small potatoes, though, compared to O'Bannion's major contribution to international terrorism, sponsored in large part by Libya.

In one of the most brilliant examples of arms diversion ever documented, he had channeled enough raw materials to allow Libyan chemists to cook up a 50-year supply of C-4 plastic explosive.

To terrorists, C-4 was like cement. It was the foundation on which their bloody trade-craft rested.

Virtually, every airport locker bomb, every booby-trapped shopping mall, every explosion that took American lives as terror left its bloody clawprint across the global map could be traced directly back to the C-4 cache sold to Libya by Miles O'Bannion.

And now, O'Bannion had engineered the acquisition of the Proteus Chain. The rogue spook was a man who didn't know when to quit. He seemed obsessed with flinging shit at America at every opportunity.

The rogue CIA operative had made a long-standing offer to the Nazi brotherhood in Latin America.

Millions would be paid for the Proteus Chain by Qaddafi. The money-hungry Spider men had finally found the offer too good to turn down. What Muammar wanted, Muammar got.

Z-Comm's primary mission was to interdict and destroy the Proteus Chain biologicals in Qaddafi's possession.

In the Mad Dog's hands, the deadly bugs of the Third Reich's lunatic experiments could do a thousand times more damage than all the C-4 in Qaddafi's terrorist arsenal and all the terror squads under his command.

While the exact nature of the Nazi CBW agents was not precisely established, it was known that at the end of World War Two the

Nazis were feverishly working on the development of a broad range of lethal viruses, bacteria, and other infectious agents.

If any of these were contained in the Proteus Chain, then Qaddafi could cheaply and all-too-effectively snuff out millions of innocent lives.

Cage had a mission of secondary priority to tackle on this op as well.

Make dogfood out of Miles O'Bannion.

As Cage listened to the American turncoat's cheerful banter on the ride into Tripoli, he realized that he was looking forward to it.

In fact, it would make his day.

FOURTEEN

Sam Proffit had already arrived in Tripoli a week prior to Domino and Cage. Posing as a Canadian drifter, Proffit had carried a passport showing a long string of departures and arrivals from countries stretching from southern Europe to the Middle East.

While North Americans were regarded with overt hostility in Libya, as elsewhere in the Arab world, Canadians were at least tolerated.

Proffit had taken a French air shuttle from Paris to Algiers. He'd had no trouble getting through one of the Libyan border checkpoints from Algeria, especially after bribing the border guards. Flashy, high-tech electronics were worth their weight in gold in the Third World.

They were the modern equivalent of wampum. The Dutch had gotten Manhattan Island for a string of beads. Proffit was able to penetrate the terrorist mecca of the world by trading a couple of micro-TVs for the silence of the corrupt border guards.

By the time Cage and Domino had touched down at the airport, Proffit was already at work at his new job as a dishwasher at a well-known restaurant in central Tripoli called the Hegira.

He had walked into the restaurant one day, looking for work after being turned down by several other merchants in the business district.

Fortunately, a dishwasher had just been fired at this particular eatery and Proffit had been hired on the spot. Anybody checking on how the tow-headed drifter had come to work at the Hegira restaurant would have discovered nothing very irregular.

What they would have not discovered was that Hamdi, the restaurant's owner, was a man opposed to the present political situation in his country.

The restaurant owner detested Daffy Qaddafi and the fanatic cabal of scum sheiks who ran the nation. Hamdi was of Bedouin descent. When the colonel had taken power in a military coup in 1969, Hamdi's tribe had found itself squatters on their own land. Land that would soon be underwater.

Qaddafi had had big plans for the country, plans that Allah's blessing of the river of oil that flowed beneath the desert sands would make a reality. Skyscrapers would be raised where only the tents of shepherds had stood before. Modern cities would rise majestically from the shifting desert sands.

So would dams. This particular dam had forced Hamdi to leave his ancestral home forever.

Proffit was given a small room above the restaurant that overlooked the narrow, twisting street filled with squatting beggars, mangy dogs, and dirty children in filthy rags. There was a sink with hot and cold running insects and a broken mirror above the sink. The toilet was down the hall.

Across from his window was a mosque from which he could hear the hysterical chanting of the faithful as they prayed to Allah five times a day. In between, recorded blessings blared from a loudspeaker at passersby in the street.

The wind that blew in through the window felt like it had spent time in a pizza oven. But Proffit wasn't concerned with the lack of air-conditioning. Or the smells. The important thing was that the top floor room was reasonably safe from prying eyes, and within easy access of the roof for an emergency getaway if that became necessary.

The room would become Z-Comm's communication nerve center for the duration of the op.

The core of the system was a sophisticated piece of commo gear, an MR64 burst transmitter that could bounce a signal off a Ryolite-class Intelsat in high geosynchronous orbit which could be received up to half a continent away.

The unit itself very closely resembled a laptop computer, except that it was encased in a hardened steel shell painted a military olive drab. While older models relied for storage on cassette tape prior to transmission, the MR64 was state-of-the-art, with a capacity of up to 720 k-bytes of text in RAM memory. A keystroke would delete even lengthy transmissions from memory. The MR64 also had automatic encryption capability so that one-time code pads were no longer necessary for the sender.

The commo man operated the unit by typing his message in at the unit's keyboard. The digitized message was then encoded and electronically compressed by transmission in a single high-intensity pulse that lasted only a microsecond. The sender could throw the message on the supertwist screen, in code or in clear, for revision before transmission.

High-speed transmission via the burst principle made a signal extremely hard to detect, even with the sophisticated ECCM (electronic counter-countermeasures) technology now on line. While the presence of a burst would almost certainly be detected on the sensitive equipment of intelligence listening posts, its point of origin would be almost impossible to pinpoint with any degree of accuracy.

Proffit would relay info from Cage and Domino in Tripoli to Zabriskie and Bear in Chad and vice versa. If they could locate the Proteus Chain, they would report it to him and he would instantly relay the intel to Bear and Zabriskie, stationed across the border in Chad. Proffit also had the responsibility of backing Cage and Domino up. That included tackling the nuts and bolts of extraction from Tripoli when the target had been identified and located.

The team would then link up and smash the Libyan death lab in a SLAM raid. Likewise, if the op went bad, Proffit could flash a precoded distress signal which would instantly mobilize a Chadian rescue chopper to fly toward a rally point in the Libyan desert.

If all went well, though, the operation would unfold in three phases.

Search.

Locate.

Annihilate.

And extract from the strike zone before the dust of combat settled.

Almost five hundred miles away, at a clandestine military base in Northern Chad, the two members of Z-Comm not inside Libya were engaged in a tactical problem of another sort—what to do with themselves through the long wait that lay ahead.

Zabriskie and MacBeth were sitting on an arsenal of sophisticated weaponry and ordnance in preparation for the coming blitzkreig inside the den of the Libyan lion. But how long it would be before the mission jelled was anyone's guess at this point.

The base was used as a forward observation post in the on-again, off-again war with Qaddafi's forces that marked the uneasy truce between the small black African republic and the large Islamic state to its north.

The base occupied a zone of desert at the foot of a craggy mountain range that formed a natural barrier between the two warring nations.

During the day, the temperature rose to as high as 120 degrees fahrenheit. At night, it plunged severely, to a frigid 40 degrees, and occasionally went below freezing.

Their only company was their liaison officer with the Chadian army, a Captain Jaloub. Jaloub was a tall black man with a penchant for bad jokes.

He was also beating Bear and Zabriskie at five-card stud. They had figured the guy to be an amateur at the American card game. Until, that is, he'd looked up from a winning hand and casually asked them if they'd ever been to Las Vegas. Where he'd worked as a croupier at Caesar's Palace.

Posing as the arms dealer and his mistress, Cage and Domino enjoyed the hospitality of the renegade CIA operative.

Qaddafi had rewarded the American expatriate in the style of a feudal baron. O'Bannion was sitting pretty in a villa in the Sharifa Heights overlooking the exclusive Al-Maquer section of Tripoli, a district reserved for the rich and the powerful.

The hilltop villa with a magnificent view of the seacoast was reached by turning off the main highway onto a long, narrow, gravel-topped drive that mazed through groves of wild fig and olive trees that had grown on the former French estate for over a century.

At the end of the drive stood a magnificent colonial mansion, its interior opulently appointed in the finest imported chrome-and-leather Bauhaus furnishings.

Abstract canvases and framed art deco posters hung on the walls, beside glass display cases filled with bizarre pre-Columbian carvings and classical Greek pottery lit by Tizio floorlamps.

A huge Patmos rug decorated with geometric shapes covered the polished teak-wood floor of the main dining room, which was dominated by an enormous mahogany table.

Their host had given his guests a sumptuous visitors' suite. Clearly, the Libyans were extending the red carpet treatment to the man they believed to be the key to matching the Proteus Chain biologicals with weapons-delivery systems.

High picture windows opened onto a veranda which overlooked a swimming pool set in a terrace on the side of a hill inlaid with zodiacal mosaics. The pool was shaped like a giant palm tree.

Beyond the pool, and in contrast to the gaudiness of O'Bannion's contemporary showplace, gleamed the ancient, needle-peaked domes of whitewashed mosques and the stark modern structures of downtown Tripoli that rose into the searing afternoon sky above narrow, filthy alleys crisscrossed by clotheslines flapping in the burning desert wind.

Cage and Domino combed the VIP suite for concealed surveillance devices, doing the best they could in the absence of electronic-bug-detectors. Such gear, like the presence of weapons, would mark them as something other than the people they claimed to be, and that they couldn't afford.

They discovered two subminiature voice pickups. One had been concealed in the navel of a nude in an expressionist painting that hung on the walls. The other was behind a wall switch. Worst-casing it told them there were certainly several more in the suite.

Cage and Domino also found a fiber-optics tube mounted unobtrusively in one high corner of the bedroom wall.

With a sensor tip no wider than the circumference of a dime, the fiber-optics tube could give a remote viewing station a wide-angle view of the bedroom as good as or better than a conventional surveillance videocam.

It had been placed, Cage noted with a grin, so that whoever was watching them could get a good view of what went on in the four-poster bed in the center of the bedroom.

O'Bannion stood in the darkness a few doors from the guest suite studying the TV surveillance monitors.

Cloede and the girl showed up clearly as they unpacked and looked around the room. The fiber optics were practically a God-given gift to spooks. When Cloede was with the Company, stuff like that was science fiction. Audio surveillance alone had a lot of drawbacks.

With the fiber optics you could stick a camera practically right up their assholes and they wouldn't know it.

Once you had the fuckers on TV you had them dead bang. There was no way they were going to wriggle out of whatever shit you caught them doing.

And once you had them by the balls, their hearts and minds followed. Erlichman always did have a way with words, O'Bannion reflected.

O'Bannion watched as Cloede lay down on

the bed and smoked a cigaret while the girl undressed and went into the shower.

She really did have a sensational body, the spook had to admit—great tits, flat belly, hard, tight ass—even if she had a wardrobe that would make Dolly Parton gag and puke. O'Bannion watched Domino go into the bathroom and come out with towels wrapped around her body and hair.

The rogue CIA man turned up the sensitivity on the concealed microphones he'd placed inside the visitor suite. Listening, he could detect no hint in their conversation that they knew about the surveillance devices in the suite.

This could mean that Cloede and the girl were in fact who they claimed to be.

Then again, it might indicate that they were smart enough operatives to "sheep-dip" their covers, completely losing themselves in their role-playing. His men had already gone over their bags with everything from x-rays to electronic bomb-sniffers and discovered nothing out of the ordinary.

As soon as Cloede and his mistress left the suite, O'Bannion's men would go over their carry-on belongings too.

Every item would be put through a fine-meshed security sieve. Every stitch of clothing would be thoroughly checked out. Toiletries and drugs would be painstakingly inspected for everything from hidden transmitters to concealed explosives.

Each personal effect would be examined with the utmost scrutiny, treated with the utmost caution.

O'Bannion was not going to let himself get caught with his dick in the ointment. If his two houseguests turned out to be dirty, then he would know it and know it soon.

Of course, O'Bannion didn't expect to find any smoking guns whether they were who they claimed to be or were intelligence operatives sent in to stage a black-bag job.

Either way, it was a sure bet that their personal effects would turn out to be squeaky clean.

If they were ringers, then they would expect to be thoroughly searched, in which case they'd be savvy enough not to break tradecraft with out-of-character personal effects.

If they were bona fide, then they would have no reason to be carrying anything out of the ordinary.

Still, O'Bannion hadn't stayed alive in the brutal dog-eat-dog of espionage because he neglected to check out every angle.

The spook played the deadly game by the rules, and the rules said to accept nothing at face value. O'Bannion would methodically check out Cloede and his squeeze just as standard procedure dictated, even though he knew in advance that nothing conclusive would turn up.

Although the security checks with the

Italians and Americans that O'Bannion had run through the Libyan Moukhabarat or intelligence service had come up negative on Cloede and the girl, there was still something in the back of the spook's mind that was flashing a warning signal about his two guests.

He couldn't put his finger on what it was yet, though. But that would come.

It always did.

O'Bannion had learned long ago to trust his hunches. They were never wrong. His first hunch was always the right one. And his hunch about Cloede was that the arms dealer might just be a fucking ringer.

Maybe it was something in those eyes or that smile. Yeah, he thought. The smile was the thing. It was, it was . . . the word that finally came to him was *predatory*. That, of course, could be perfectly natural in the line of work that Cloede was in. Then again, it might be a giveaway to an operation going down.

One way or another, O'Bannion would find out the truth. He would continue checking into Cloede's background and the girl's as well. If they were running an op, then somewhere, somehow, there would be a joker in the deck.

Eventually they would slip up, break tradecraft. Even the slightest mistake would tell him all he needed to know.

O'Bannion would have people waiting for that moment.

Watching and waiting for Cloede or his girlfriend to make a wrong move.

And if they did, or more than likely, *when* they did, O'Bannion would blow them down the black hole of eternity.

As casually as blowing a fart out the hole in his ass.

FIFTEEN

"Have yourself a ball, baby," the goateed "arms-broker" told the dumb blonde as he exited the stretch and tucked his head inside to receive a chaste peck on the lips from Domino. "Buy whatever you want," Cage went on. "The sky's the limit."

"I can't wait to break in my new American Express card," Domino gushed, laying on the schmaltz as thick as her eyeliner. "Is there really any good shopping in this town?" she cooed at O'Bannion in a voice that could turn steel to butter. "I mean, Tripoli reminds me a lot of Reno and I know there's great shopping in Reno, so why shouldn't there be great shopping in Tripoli too? Am I making sense?" Domino batted her eyes and smiled.

"Sure," the spook returned with a sly wink

at Cage. "My chauffeur will take you to the swankiest shops in Tripoli. He knows them all. What especially interests you? Rugs? Fine glassware? Maybe furniture?"

Domino giggled and flashed the rogue intelligence man a smile he could feel in his hip pocket. "Well," she said more breathily than Monroe ever did, "some sexy lingerie for openers. Lucky is getting tired of the old peekaboo nighties I've been wearing since Paris. I mean, he's only able to get it up twice a night now."

O'Bannion cleared his throat before answering. Cage fought to keep a straight face as he watched the freelance operative's beefy face redden. "Yeah, well, uh . . . I'm sure Saheen will know exactly where to take you, ma'am."

"Don't you want us to pick you up when you're finished with that important meeting of yours?" Domino asked sweetly. "After all, I don't want to hog this big beautiful chariot." She ran her fingers along the upholstery. "Oooh, this leather feels so good I could just, I don't know, *masturbate* or something."

"That's okay, honey," O'Bannion returned with a smile. "We can get ourselves back to the villa okay. Besides, this meeting might take a while."

Domino blew Cage kisses and waved as the limo drove off. Cage waved back at the smoked rear windshield of the rapidly rolling stretch as it turned a palm-fringed corner and disappeared down a narrow, twisting street barely wider than the limo itself was.

"That's some hot piece of fluff you got there, Lucky," O'Bannion told Cage. "She as good in the sack as she advertises or does that lady promise more than she delivers?"

Cage wrapped his arm around O'Bannion's broad shoulders. O'Bannion tensed as Cage used the opportunity to strongarm the scumbag a little, but tried not to let on.

Cage felt an instant animosity, as though he'd just picked up a rock and felt something slimy crawl up his fingers. O'Bannion's body gave off the vinegary odor of sweat.

It would be easy to snuff the spook. So fast and so simple. A hard twist of the neck and it would all be over for the American renegade.

But that would have to come later if it came at all. Cage had more important matters to take care of first. Priority one was to locate the whereabouts of the Proteus Chain so its site of the Nazi germ cache could be targeted for incendiary destruction by the rest of the Z-Comm demolition force.

Once that was out of the way, there'd be time to deal with O'Bannion.

It would be the icing on the cake.

"I never go with a loser," Cage returned with a smile, looking into O'Bannion's shit-brown eyes.

Then he walked up the stairs that led to the entranceway of the Libyan Ministry of Defense.

Turning in midstep, he said as though in afterthought, "Maybe I'll let you watch sometime."

Proffit negotiated the twists and turns of the narrow, sunbaked streets of Tripoli's Old Quarter as surely as any of the robed natives who passed him on their silent journeys to only Allah knew where.

His destination was a small shop located in an out-of-the-way section of the city that sold curios, old books of Koranic lore, and secondhand musical instruments.

There was a man whom he was to meet there who had some information for him. He was a shopkeeper in the Old Quarter whose son had done work on the Jalu oil fields near a newly built military installation at 'Uqba bin Nafi.

From its description, the 'Uqba bin Nafi military base was of the right dimensions for the lab Z-Comm was searching for. A four-story building at the base was off-limits to all personnel without security clearances.

Most importantly, there had recently been an explosion at the base in which several workers were killed. Men in white suits had been called in to sweep the area. This jibed with procedure for mopping up a CBW accident.

In time, the maze of narrow alleys through which Proffit passed opened onto a small public square. A bubbling stone fountain stood at its center. Clustering around it, veiled Arab women filled large plastic jugs from its multiple streams while ragged children cavorted at their skirts, taunting an emaciated dog that had wandered up looking for a handout.

The shop that was Proffit's destination stood on the far side of the public fountain. Its sign, in both Arabic and French as many in Tripoli, advertised the wares that sat on dusty shelves behind a flyspecked plate-glass window. Proffit pushed through the door into the cool, musty darkness beyond, hearing a small bell tinkle as the door shut behind him.

The shop's dark interior smelled of moldering paper and decades of piled-up dust. Musical instruments of various kinds hung from the walls above shelves crammed cheek-by-jowl with old volumes and used paperbacks. Glass display cases containing cheap ceramic figurines, glass trinkets, and other souvenir items were haphazardly crowded up against one another.

A wizened old man wearing a white turban with a face that was the color and texture of cracked leather and wire-rim spectacles with thick round lenses stood behind a counter near the entrance to the shop. The shopkeeper wore an open-necked polyester shirt. Behind the old man was an open doorway through which Proffit could see a small kitchen. The spicy odor of *couscous* cooking on the stove wafted out of the kitchen, and a large orange cat jumped to the countertop as Proffit approached.

"I'm here for the figurine I phoned about," Proffit told the shopkeeper in English as he stroked the cat's fur, hearing the animal immediately begin to purr contentedly.

The shopkeeper's large, dark eyes stared back at him from behind the thick lenses. Proffit noticed sweat beading his high brow and upper lip.

"You have come from far for this figurine?" the old man returned, giving Proffit the prearranged recognition code. Proffit nodded.

"The figurine is for my uncle, a collector of rare and unique items."

The old man reached beneath the glass countertop and placed a small porcelain cobra atop it. The figurine was painted a dull black, its eyes were glittering red zircons. Proffit noticed that the old man's hands trembled as he slid the cobra toward him, just as he caught the flicker of movement behind him reflected in the glass-topped counter.

"There is no charge for—"

Grabbing the cobra, Proffit ducked just as the silenced East German wz63 SMG belched a burst of 9-mm hollowpoints from behind the old man. The cat hissed and leapt onto one of the shelves, sending objects flying as it fled from harm's way. Part of the autoburst had caught the old man's head. The corpse slumped forward, its hands dangling over the edge of the desk, its white turban discolored by a spreading red blotch.

Two swarthy Moukhabarat agents in shiny gray suits raced from the kitchen behind the desk, throwing lead from the wz63 full-auto blasters in their fists. Proffit was in the shop somewhere, they knew. He hadn't made the street yet. If he had, then the men that were posted outside would have fired already. Guns at the ready, they cautiously crept through the shop, playing a lethal game of terminal tag.

Suddenly one of the Arab fastgunners heard the cat hiss, and reflexively flicked his gaze to the streak of orange flashing past his shoes. The momentary lapse cost him his life. The next thing he knew, something had exploded in his heart. The two razor-sharp ebony horns of the Berber ceremonial mask that Proffit had thrown had skewered the Arab right through his chest. Blood spurted thickly from his nose and mouth.

Proffit dodged out of the shop as the second Libyan gunman opened fire. But the Libyan was pinned by the body of the first zapper. The backups outside in the plaza pushed aside women at the fountain as they tried to draw beads, but the pulsebeat was enough for Proffit to spring back into the maze of streets that led away from the Old Quarter of the city. As he ran he could hear them curse and holler behind him.

He looked back. Two shapes had entered

the maze after him. Proffit shimmied up a drainpipe and climbed in through an open window. Shoe leather slapping concrete echoed in the alley below him. Suddenly, Proffit heard shouting in the room behind him. A big guy in saffron robes was coming at him, brandishing a long, curving scimitar of some kind, obviously mad at the uninvited company.

Silhouetted against the whitewashed walls of the ancient buildings, the two intelligence men had drawn pistols and broken into a run at the sound of the swordsman's bellow of rage in the apartment above them. Pistol shots shattered the lock on the thick wooden door.

Proffit wrestled the Arab sword-swinger off him. He fell down the stairs, bowling the Libyan shooters over on their way up. Proffit ran up to the attic and punched out a skylight. The roofscape was clear. He jumped a narrow alley. In minutes he was many streets away.

Climbing back down to street level, Proffit hightailed it out of the Old Quarter back to the Hegira restaurant. Dodging into the patrons' toilet and locking the door, he unrolled the pill of paper that he had found behind a plug of wood that came out of the bottom of the cobra figurine.

It was a hand-drawn map of an intallation in the Libyan desert. Over the installation whoever had prepared it had drawn the image of a skull and crossbones. Proffit memorized the map and flushed the paper down the toilet.

The Libyan Defense Minister was a small, wiry man in a military uniform who chain-smoked Turkish cigarets as he spoke about the glorious mission of Libya.

The Defense Minister, named Nuri El-Kamal, looked too diminutive for the huge desk he sat behind in an oversized wingback executive chair. On the wall beside the Defense Minister hung an enormous framed portrait of Colonel Muammar Qaddafi, resplendent in a gaudy white uniform, mirror-lensed aviators hiding his eyes.

Cage sat on one of the comfortable leather chairs facing the desk beside O'Bannion. The renegade CIA man appeared bored, but Cage was aware that beneath the unconcerned front there was a tension so taut it almost hummed.

They had been discussing the procurement of American Stinger missile systems. The man-portable antiarmor rocket had been tested by the Mujahideen in Afghanistan against Russian HIND choppers.

The Stingers were also the ideal weapon for terrorist death strikes. They were light, easily transportable, and their heat-seeking warheads gave them a "fire and forget" capability that put the Stinger system many cuts above the competition—chiefly the more clumsy British Blowpipe systems that relied on the firer to remotely guide the warhead in flight.

In the hands of Terrorist International, the lethal firepower of advanced Stinger technology could mean suicide raids on a far greater and deadlier scale then ever before. The interest of the Libyans in acquiring Stingers meant that a possible resurgence of high-visibility terrorist ops was being planned by the Mad Dog of the Middle East.

"How soon can you arrange for a sample of the weapons?" El-Kamal asked Cage. "As a gesture of good faith."

Cage told the Libyan Defense honcho that a Stinger system could be on its way as early as the following week. There would be strings attached, though, Cage added. After Iran-Contra, the U.S. Defense Department had tightened up on end-user certificates. These had once been routinely ignored by arms dealers, so that sophisticated arms destined for anti-U.S. regimes could be brokered via friendly third-party countries who played both sides of the street. It was a lot tougher now, Cage explained.

"I'm not only interested in turning a profit," the "arms-broker" told El-Kamal. "I want something more from your end."

"And what might this 'something else' be?" the Libyan asked cautiously.

"It's no secret that your country routinely provides bases for the training of, shall we say, various paramilitary units," Cage replied with just the right hint of a smile—

not enough to offend, just enough to look conspiratorial.

"I need an isolated training base for a unit of my own. I can assure you, however, that this particular operation will not in any way involve your country or compromise its intelligence resources. Its purpose would be of a purely mercenary nature." Cage smiled more broadly now, his accent on the word *mercenary* emphasizing its double meaning as El-Kamal nodded in understanding. "In short I would like to be able to have a look around for potential sites for this training camp."

Now it was the Libyan's turn to smile. Leaning back in his chair, he glanced at the American turncoat for a moment. It was obvious that Cloede was planning a major criminal operation of some kind. If so, then there would be the potential of blackmailing the arms broker for even greater concessions in the future. Cloede would be provided with his training base and anything else he wanted. The base would be placed under 24-hour surveillance. The Libyans might even insist on a share of whatever it was that Cloede's operation netted him.

"I think something can be worked out," El-Kamal told Cage. "I will make arrangements for a military helicopter to be placed at your disposal for inspection of any sites you wish." The Libyan Defense Minister leaned forward and stared at Cage over steepled hands. "Is that satisfactory, Mr. Cloede?"

Cage smiled back at the Libyan.

"Most satisfactory, Colonel," he answered, extending his hand and shaking El-Kamal's.

Cage also told the Libyan that he would personally demonstrate the capability of the advanced Stinger for Libyan brass. This pleased the Defense Minister. He smiled and hit Cage with the clincher.

"Mr. Cloede," the Libyan began, "we are most interested in the Stingers, but what we wish most is something else besides. Are you familiar with the American Bigeye program?"

At the mention of Bigeye, Cage felt an almost electric spark come off O'Bannion. Instantly, he knew that the Stingers were only a test.

Bigeye was the code name for a new generation of chemical-biological weapons under development by the Pentagon. The bombs were designed to provide highly effective delivery of CBW agents. They could be launched from rockets or dropped from planes. They could also be delivered as cluster bomblets, in the form of aerial submunitions.

"Yes, certainly," Cage told El-Kamal. "But the Bigeye bomb is not—how shall I put it—the kind of weapons system one would associate with your special tactical needs."

"Ah," El-Kamal countered immediately. "There you are wrong, Mr. Cloede."

He exhaled creamy Turkish smoke and

leaned forward on his wingback chair, steepling his arms and staring hard at Cage.

"Libya is interested in all weapons technologies. It is an open secret that we already have nuclear capability. Not that we would ever use it as an aggressor," he quickly added, "but it is a capability that we must use in our own defense. The Americans, the Zionists, even our Arab brethren could attack at any moment. We must be prepared."

O'Bannion leaned forward, adding, "Specifically, the Minister is concerned with the Iraqis. As I'm sure you know, they used chemical weapons in their war with Iran. Like it or not, the Middle East might well turn into the world's first proving ground for CBW weapons on a massive scale. The Libyans want to make sure that they have the technological edge in that combat theater, way ahead of what anybody else has." O'Bannion added, "This is purely defensive."

El-Kamal added with a curt nod, "Yes, purely for defense. We Libyans are a peace-loving peoplc, Mr. Cloede. We are never the aggressor."

"I'll see what I can do," Cage told them. The meeting was as good as positive confirmation that Libya was in possession of the Proteus Chain and actively producing it in large quantities.

All they needed now would be the means of delivering the deady bugs to targets.

Zabriskie and Bear set up their burst

transmitter unit. It was getting close to Proffit's prearranged transmission time.

The unit was set out in the open air on a small table, large enough to support the compact keyboard and miniature printer for hard copy of the coded transmission.

Zabriskie also had a one-time code pad that would allow him to quickly translate the encrypted printout into understandable English.

Zabriskie activated the unit and waited as it automatically locked onto the Big Bird Intelsat that passed overhead in geosynchronous orbit, many miles in space.

The unit's indicator light flashed that the signal had been received. It took only a second. Zabriskie hit a few keystrokes and the small thermal printer began emitting tiny mosquitolike sounds as the printhead zipped across the paper at high speed.

Less than two minutes later, the printer went off line as the hard copy was completed. Zabriskie tore off the final page, and while MacBeth and Captain Jaloub looked on, deciphered the encrypted message with the one-time code pad.

When it had been decoded, the message read that Proffit and Cage had found evidence of the existence of the Proteus Chain in a lab a few hundred miles out of Tripoli in the Sahara desert and that the Nazi CBWs were now in mass production.

SIXTEEN

The French Super Frelon helicraft darted low over the Libyan desert. Thermal currents buffeted the combat chopper as it passed across rows of undulating sand dunes, making the helo dip and rise unpredictably in the sudden patches of turbulence.

Mirrored Ray Bans protected Cage's eyes against the searing rays of the North African sun as he sat in the copilot's seat and watched the helo's insectlike shadow float with ghostly stillness across the arid wasteland below them that was broken only by remote roads and occasional palm-fringed wadis.

Below, to the left of the helicopter, Cage could see the sunwashed concrete blockhouses that made up the 'Uqba bin Nafi military research facility.

'Uqba bin Nafi perfectly matched the requirements for a CBW research installation. For one thing, it was miles from the nearest village or major highway, accessible only by chopper or land vehicle capable of sustained desert travel. Its remoteness would be a necessity for the containment of any deadly germ agents that might otherwise escape the laboratories to contaminate nearby population centers.

For another, there was a mobile installation of Soviet SAM antiaircraft missiles on the facility. It didn't make sense that Soviet surface-to-air missiles would be deployed outside the installation unless the Libyans considered it a possible target for an air strike launched by a hostile power. Since the April 1986 bombing of Tripoli by U.S. F111s, the Libyans had paid special attention to air defense for priority targets.

"What's that military base over there?" Cage asked the chopper pilot, pointing toward the installation. Although he already knew the answer, Cage wanted to know how much he could pump the pilot for.

"This is 'Uqba bin Nafi base," the pilot returned in English that was laced with a British accent, like most speakers of the language in the region. " 'Uqba bin Nafi small army base, not important."

Cage smiled. "How about we swing around for a closer look at it?"

"We do not have clearance for such

maneuver," the Libyan pilot returned. "You see SAMs down there? They shoot down helicopter if we fly over. Soldiers do not care if we are part of the same army or not."

The pilot managed a small laugh. "So we had better continue to our destination straightaway," he answered again.

"If it's such a small, unimportant base," Cage pressed the pilot, "then why all the SAMs?"

The pilot smiled again. "I do not make the rules," he replied lamely. "I am only required to follow them. I am afraid you must ask my superiors these questions."

About 25 minutes of flying time later, the Super Frelon was setting down on its skids in a remote stretch of desert about 50 miles east of 'Uqba bin Nafi. Another chopper was already there.

Ducking the rotorwash amid a cloud of dust whipped up by the rapidly spinning blades, Cage climbed out of the cockpit. Moments later the French-built Super Frelon lifted off again and banked sharply, growing smaller until it vanished completely from sight.

· An assortment of Libyan military brass and political leaders in mufti sat in rows of folding chairs that looked out of place in the middle of the sandy nowhere. In front of Cage, propped on a collapsible tripod, was the Stinger man-portable antiarmor missile unit that had been delivered through channels to Libyan agents.

The Stinger unit had arrived in Tripoli a few days before. Despite recent bipartisan hearings on the Iran arms diversion scam and an end-user certificate listing its destination as Honduras, the Stinger had been covertly transported through middlemen in Tegucigalpa, where a CIA proprietary airline had shuttled it to the coast of Corsica in crates marked, "farm equipment."

Despite outrage over unsanctioned arms sales to Iran, there was nothing unethical about baiting a terrorist trap with U.S. weapons. You want to catch rats, you put out cheese. You want to catch terrorists, you dangle some high-tech hardware in their faces.

Cage shook hands with O'Bannion and the Defense Minister, who had risen from their seats in the gallery to greet him as he stepped from the Super Frelon.

After he'd glad-handed the assembled brass in similar fashion, Cage got down to the nitty-gritty. Hefting the man-portable Stinger rig to his shoulder, he armed the laser-augmented heat-seaking warhead. Sighting through the glowing red LCD reticle he prepared to trigger the round.

Signaling to O'Bannion that he was ready, Cage waited until the target helicopter lifted off the nearby launch pad and began performing a series of zigzagging evasive maneuvers at an altitude of 30 feet. Ordinarily a remote-piloted drone ship would be used to demo the Stinger. But this was Libya.

There were no shortage of fanatic pilots only too glad to die for Allah.

When the Stinger's laser target-acquisition system had locked onto the chopper, Cage studded the warhead's firing system.

The high-explosive rocket whooshed from the launch tube leaving behind a contrail of white smoke to mark its zigzagging flight path as it flew on an intercept vector toward the wildly careening chopper.

Three seconds later, the missile's heat-seeking sensor homed in on the chopper's engine and it scored a direct hit. A ball of fire blossomed over the desert as the helo completely disintegrated. Cage threw the empty Stinger firing tube to the ground.

"Most impressive," the Defense Minister said, approaching him. The Libyan lit up a cheroot and took a deep drag, watching the flaming bits of debris patter the desert, where they lay smoldering. "There is, after all, nothing quite like American goods."

"I hope the guy who flew that bird appreciates that fact," Cage said.

El-Kamal smiled.

"Right now he is being welcomed into *Behesht Zahra,* our Islamic Paradise, by a hundred beautiful courtesans who will give him as much kif as he can smoke and as much pleasure as he can stand." The Defense Minister stared up into the cobalt sky as if he were looking in on the party. "He has far better things on his mind now."

O'Bannion's villa was the scene of a lavish party to celebrate the closing of the arms deal that would put U.S. Stingers in Libyan hands. A quarter-of-a-million-dollar down payment had been deposited into "Cloede's" bank account as an advance on a dozen Stinger missiles, with the balance due on delivery. There was also a Libyan option on another dozen systems if the first shipment proved acceptable.

Lebanese hashish and Scotch booze flowed in the American turncoat's Tripoli villa like dirty water from an overflowing commode. The many rooms of the colonial mansion were crowded with an assortment of VIPs, mostly foreign dignitaries from the renegade nations of the Third World who still maintained embassies in the Mad Dog's backyard nation.

For those who desired it, there were other diversions in rooms off the main ballroom. Hard drugs, women, even young boys were available there. Of course, all the goings-on in these chambers of delight would be captured on hidden video cameras for later use in persuading those who had danced to Libyan music that it was now time to pay the piper.

Cage and Domino were the center of attention. The bogus arms broker had scored big with the Libyans. He was now in with the out-crowd. O'Bannion had just introduced the tuxedo'd Cage to an Iraqi general who wondered aloud if Cage could get his country some Stingers too. Cage felt like handing out numbers. It seemed like these Third World assholes had nothing on their minds but blowing each other to hell.

A turbaned servant came up to O'Bannion and whispered in his master's ear.

The expatriate CIA man excused himself and left the ballroom clutching his martini glass.

He went into his study and closed the door. Standing on a zebra rug before a gilt-wood Regency desk, he flipped on a Tizio lamp resembling a falcon in flight. Framed within the cone of cyan light he took the receiver from its cradle. The phone call was from the chief of the Libyan intelligence agency, Moukhabarat al-Wazir.

"I thought I should phone you with this right away," the spook sheik told the free-lance hitter.

"What is it?"

"The man you know as Cloede," the man from Moukhabarat said on the other end. "He is, as you Americans say, a 'ringer.' Of this we have positive confirmation."

O'Bannion's grip tightened so hard on the receiver that his knuckles turned white. "Who is he?"

"We don't know this yet," the oily voice on the other end of the line returned. "But we do know he is definitely not Cloede."

There was the sound of pages being riffled on the other end of the telephone line. "The real Cloede died in a Swiss hospital a few hours ago. The cause was congestive heart failure. An agent in our employ at the hospital was able to identify the body as it was being surreptitiously moved from the clinic through a little-used rear entrance. Apparently there was an attempt made to keep the real Cloede out of the picture so your man could carry out his mission, whatever that might be."

O'Bannion was silent for a long moment, his nostrils flaring as he breathed deeply and rhythmically. When he was in control again, he picked up the martini glass and downed the rest of the clear liquid inside it, tasting nothing.

"Let me know as soon as you hear anything," he said softly into the mouthpiece and hung up the phone.

Then he took a 9-mm Makarov automatic from a drawer, switched off the desk lamp, and left the study with the small, deadly handgun hidden in the pocket of his white tux.

The busy restaurant was packed with a noisy crowd watching a belly dancer weave from table to table undulating her oiled midriff and clicking the small cymbals she held between thumb and forefinger. On the club's small stage, a five-man band played a fast instrumental with a hypnotic beat to which the belly dancer timed her rhythmic gyrations.

The music and the shouts and whistles of

the audience reached into the hot kitchen next to the dining area where Proffit was up to his armpits in a sink full of dirty dishes. The noise of the Arab party animals didn't prevent him from spotting the three guys in cheap suits who'd just come into the kitchen and headed straight for him.

Grabbing a humongous pot of boiling water from the stove beside him, Proffit sent it flying at the Libyan first ratprick. The guy's screams of agony were muffled by the enormous kettle over his head as he thrashed around with second-degree burns all over his face and head.

His two pards dipped for their blasters, but Proffit had already leapfrogged a table and grabbed hold of one of the lighting fixtures that hung from the high tin ceiling on galvanized link chains.

He swung across the tables of food and over the heads of cursing kitchen staffers, who ducked as 9-mm zappers crisscrossed the kitchen, and made a two-point landing in front of the swinging kitchen doors.

Body-checking the swinging doors, Proffit was out on the floor of the crowded restaurant. The belly dancer suddenly turned and lunged at Proffit with a long, curved dagger she had whipped from somewhere in her skimpy costume.

Grabbing up a big tray heaped with broiled camel meat, Proffit deflected the dagger, simultaneously grabbing the belly dancer and hurling her into the bandstand, where she crashed head-on through the skin of a kettle drum.

Parabellums whined behind him like banshees as one of the hitters let fly a 9-mm fusilade. Proffit grabbed a flaming shish-kabob skewer from a wheeled cart and pitched the long metal needle at the Arab shooter. The flaming skewer buried itself in his left eyeball, and the gunman crashed backward into a large potted cactus, then out through a plate-glass window, where he came to rest beside an old beggar who immediately began to go through his pockets.

Panic now took hold of the Hegira restaurant as diners stampeded en masse for the single entrance. One of the tables was on fire and the sprinkler system doused the entire place with water. Patrons used chairs to smash the big front window and spilled out into the street. Proffit ducked out the dining-room entrance and took the single flight to his upstairs room two steps at a time.

Locking the door behind him, he grabbed the burst transmitter from its hiding place under a pile of what might well rank as the dirtiest laundry in human history, the last place he figured anybody would look.

A special emergency frequency had been prearranged by Z-Comm for transmission of a distress signal. It would be necessary to transmit in the clear, but that didn't matter now anyway. The scum sheiks already had his position. The clear signal would be transmitted on an open frequency that was monitored at all times by Zabriskie and Bear at the Chadian forward observation base at Tarso Ourari.

Proffit keyed in the distress code and hit the send key.

Racing to the closet, he unrolled the large rug he'd bought at a local shop, grabbed the khaki rucksack stashed inside it, and slung it over his shoulder. The rucksack was Proffit's "just in case." It contained several taken-down assault weapons and grenades. Just in case.

Proffit climbed out the window and pitched a FRAG grenade into the room, ducking to one side as the blast blew the Moukhabarat rats who'd just busted in straight to Islamic mutt heaven.

Then he climbed down the drainpipe into the narrow alley running alongside the building.

Holding a snifter of brandy, Cage was in the middle of a conversation with a Soviet embassy official who was running down the top 40 five-year plans of all time when he saw trouble heading his way in the form of O'Bannion and two beefy brackets with howitzer-sized bulges under their jackets. Cage needed a quick diversion.

"Excuse me, guy," he said, pouring his brandy over the Russkie's head and following through with a quick flick of his cigaret lighter. "But I seem to have set your head on fire."

The Russkie's fat wife screamed as her better half burst into flames and knocked over lawn furniture in a wild and sudden frenzy to take a refreshing dip in O'Bannion's pool.

While everyone at poolside watched the flame-broiled Russian beat the heat by plunging into the water, Cage was already broken-field running toward Domino, who was at the opposite end of the palm tree-shaped swimming pool.

Nice try, but still no cigar.

O'Bannion had bypassed Cage's diversion and was hustling toward him with his pair of uglies in block-and-tackle position. Cage knew they weren't coming to present him with souvenir key chains. All now had fistfuls of trouble in the form of Steyr MPi81 submachine guns.

Spotting a waiter wheeling a bar cart, Cage picked up a bottle of Jim Beam and smashed it across the guy's face. "Excuse me," he said as he hurled the cart at the onrushing phalanx of O'Bannion's shooters, "but your jaw seems to be all over my tux."

O'Bannion and his goons scattered like ninepins as the heavy cart plowed into them before upending into the pool, causing one of O'Bannion's goons to lose his balance and join the charbroiled commissar for a swim.

Nearby, Domino had already kicked off her high heels and gotten ready to rock and roll. As one of the Libyan military honchos tried to grab her, she hammered the five-inch spike heel of one patent pump into his eye. At the same time, she grabbed the 9-mm Makarov automatic holstered at his hip.

"Let's get out of here," Cage hollered as they hooked up.

"I can't run in this goddamn gown," Domino screamed. Cage grabbed a carving knife out of a haunch of virgin goat on one of the tables and slit it down the back.

"Thanks a fucking lot," she said, stripped down to bra and panties. Domino and Cage then vaulted a line of hedges surrounding the pool and ran down the sprawling grass-covered slopes of O'Bannion's estate.

"What the hell's the point, Cage?" Domino hollered as they ran. "We're in the middle of Libya, for chrissakes. Where do we go from here?"

Cage didn't have time to answer. O'Bannion had drawn a bead on him and was preparing to ventilate him with the Russkie automatic pistol.

Cage used a metal lawn chair as a shield and Domino returned fire, forcing the heavies to suck the mulch.

Snapping off bursts behind them as they ran, Domino and Cage hotfooted it for the villa's main gate. The brace of hardmen were after them again, having gotten to their feet throwing iron.

Crack!

One of the hardmen dropped. Then down went another. Cage looked behind him. The surviving hardmen were flat on the ground. Cage wondered why. Domino hadn't shot the dudes.

Then he saw Proffit standing with a night-scope-equipped Commando 5.56-mm SMG atop the stone wall that ran around the estate. Proffit waved Cage and Domino over to a small car parked outside.

Proffit climbed behind the wheel and shifted the already idling compact into gear as Cage and Domino cracked the back doors and piled inside the rear seat.

"Don't tell me," Cage told Proffit with a grin. "An Arab Hyundai dealer made you an offer you couldn't refuse."

"Nope," Proffit returned. "It was all I could boost on short notice. By the way," he said to Domino, "love that Spandex."

SEVENTEEN

With Proffit at the wheel, the Korean compact car screamed down the highway that ran past O'Bannion's villa.

The screech of tires and the roar of high-performance car engines right behind them made it clear to the Z-Commandos that whatever lead they might have on the opposition was as narrow as a flea's tear duct.

Leaning out the window, Domino and Cage hefted the weapons Proffit had brought with him on his hasty exit from the Hegira restaurant and got ready to say it with hollowpoints.

Wearing Cage's tux jacket, Domino clutched an Uzi 9-mm SMG, while Cage toted Proffit's compact Colt Commando with its

30-round staggered box mag bulging with 5.56-x-45-mm rounds.

"You think you know your way around well enough to get us out of town?" Cage wanted to know. "These streets are like a fucking maze."

"No problem," Proffit returned, swerving fast onto a narrow street little wider than the car itself. "I've got our escape route all planned out."

Cage trusted in Proffit's unerring instinct for land navigation. Proffit had a gift for mentally diagramming a place so accurately that he instantly knew it as well as the back of his hand.

Once Proffit memorized a route he never forgot it. "Last thing I did was to get off an emergency burst signal to the Bear and Harry," he told Cage and Domino. "They know where the rally point is located."

The place Proffit had in mind was a wadi about 50 miles outside of Tripoli that he'd scouted out as an emergency LZ for a heliborne rescue mission.

By now Zabriskie and MacBeth should be making final preparations for a low altitude, radar-dodging chopper run across the Sahara desert that would bring them into position for an emergency evacuation of the Tripoli penetration crew.

Proffit outlined the above to Cage and Domino as he navigated the Hyundai through the dark labyrinth of the Libyan capital's backstreets as unerringly as a human bloodhound.

Suddenly, bullets spanged off the car's rear fender. Autofire bratted from the SMGs that protruded from the windows of two Audi 500 chase vehicles that had pulled behind the Hyundai without warning. Cage and Domino returned fire instantly as Proffit ran through a series of evasive maneuvers.

So far it was just a pissing contest, though. There was still too much distance between the cars for either friendly or hostile fire to stand an even chance of scoring any kind of hit that mattered.

The status quo changed quickly as Proffit stomped on the brakes to avoid hitting an Arab in flowing robes who was crossing an intersection leading a slow-moving camel.

Proffit leaned on the horn, but it didn't do any good. The recalcitrant animal stood in the dusty street refusing to budge. In the rearview, Proffit could see the chase crews screaming down the incline of the steeply canted street.

Blitzing autofire chattered from the kill crew's hand cannons, spidering windshield glass and puncturing the car's metal skin. A ricocheting slug fragment narrowly missed Domino's head before expending itself in the cushion of the back seat.

Proffit shifted into gear and tore past the obstruction in the road, two tires on the cobblestones and the other two on a narrow margin of pavement which ended abruptly in tarp-covered scaffolding that surrounded a building undergoing renovation.

A night crew was on the scaffolding, making repairs to one of the building's walls. The scaffolding collapsed with a violently loud crash as the car's front end tore through the lightweight metal beams which supported it, bumping its way onto the road surface again with a shower of hot blue sparks as its undercarriage and transaxle collided with concrete, dirt, and stone.

Now the chase cars were right behind Z-Comm's car, their SMGs well within lethal striking range, the combined firepower of their autoweapons packing enough of a wallop to Swiss-cheese the escape car with bulletholes or send a burst of glowing steel punching through the gas tank to ignite the flammable fuel within and blow the car into eternity.

Bullets shattered the Hyundai's rear windshield as though it were made of spun candy. The windshield disintegrated into a blizzard of glass fragments that blanketed the Z-Commandos in the rear seat.

Reloading the Colt with one of the few mags remaining, Cage cleared away the jagged shards hanging from the metal frame with a few quick swipes of the SMG's metal butt.

He stuck the Commando's muzzle through the empty frame of the blown-out window, propping it on the bottom runner, and cut loose with a stuttering longburst of 5.56-mm tumblers that raked the chase car across its grille, panicking the driver into making a wild evasive swerve to the left.

The Arab wheelman almost lost control and the Audi 500 careened head-on toward the plate-glass window of a dress shop a few feet beyond the curb. The car collided with the window with the screech of tortured rubber and a cascade of disintegrating glass, and plowed right through into the store, bowling over mannequins in chic outfits and elegant evening gowns before it came to a juddering halt.

While the crew of the first chase car climbed dazedly from the wreck and struggled to push the dented vehicle back out of the window and onto the street, the second chase car shot ahead after the escape vehicle.

Rotoring fire belched from either open window as the men inside launched salvos of 9-mm autofire from the MPi81s they packed. A third shooter, standing up through the open sun-roof, cranked out .357 slugs from a Python with slow, deliberate marksmanship.

Empty shell casing leapt from the fiery breeches of the blazing autoweapons and jingled around on the floor of the speeding car.

The interior of the Audi was thick with acrid cordite fumes. Even the rush of hot, dry air through the open windows as the chase car sped after its quarry did little to dissipate the foul gray smoke and the noxious odors of overheated gunmetal from the car's interior.

As the chase entered another section of mazelike streets, the Hyundai escape car was only a few yards ahead of the pursuit vehicle still in the running. Proffit executed a series of high-speed zigzags to throw it off course while Cage and Domino poured on the gunfire.

The second car was now coming up close. In the hand of one of the men in back was a FRAG grenade.

The driver of the chase car poured on the speed.

The strategy was to pass the Hyundai and lob a grenade in through one of the windows.

Although the dangerous gambit posed a serious risk to the chase vehicle, it promised to pay a bloody dividend if it succeeded. As the driver brought the Mercedes abreast of the Hyundai's windowless rear, the guy in the shotgun seat leaned out as far as he could, his outstretched hand clutching the FRAG grenade.

With less than a foot separating the two speeding cars, he prepared to pitch the grenade into the back-seat area.

Cage triggered a 5.56-mm autoburst from the Colt SMG. A tight shot pattern struck the guy holding the grenade in the face, tearing off most of his head and splattering the driver with a spray of red glop. The deadman's corpse went into convulsions. He dropped the grenade between his legs as he pitched over backward and started thrashing around.

The man beside him frantically bent forward, searching for the dropped APERS munition that had already been activated and would explode any second.

The car behind the Hyundai went up with an earsplitting concussion, flaring into a miniature nova so bright that it was impossible to look into without blinking. The sunball lit the buildings to either side with a flickering, strobing brilliance.

Pieces of the destroyed vehicle cascaded down, peppering the cobbled street. The flaming wreckage was scattered all over the narrow thoroughfare.

The damaged second car punched through the cordon of burning wreckage with a scream of engine parts overdriven to the point of metal fatigue and a suspension system that had been pushed far beyond its limits.

But it was still on the Hyundai's tail, the shooters inside it pouring steady fire at their quarry.

Proffit swerved the escape car around a hairpin turn in the ancient street and suddenly stomped the brakes. Only a few yards up ahead, the road abruptly ended.

There was some kind of rally in progress, probably anti-American. An Arab imam in turban and flowing robe stood on a platform above the crowd shaking his fist in the air as he hollered something into a microphone.

His amplified voice thundered across the large plaza as the crowd cheered and applauded the fiery orator.

Proffit ditched the Korean compact and the three Z-Commandos hustled out and sprinted across the roadway into the crowded plaza.

The surviving chase car screeched to a halt right behind them. The activity was noticed by a trio of soldiers who had been loitering on the perimeter of the crowd watching the imam on the stage go through his routine.

Glancing behind him, Cage saw the men from the car palavering with the soldiers, who looked their way and drew their weapons as they spoke rapidly into their portable radios, calling for reinforcements.

Cage noted that one of the men from the car was O'Bannion. Their eyes locked across the crowd and each man felt the sunball of raw hatred fill their guts with fire.

Both knew their paths would cross again.

With more badguys joining the chase, Cage, Domino, and Proffit now had no choice but to elbow their way through the crowd of Libyans all around them. However psyched out by the imam's speech they might have been, and whatever their feeling toward Americans, most of the Arabs didn't feel like arguing with the automatic weapons the Z-crew packed.

A couple of ragheads, though, had other ideas.

Two camel-fuckers whipped long, curved

swords from their flowing robes and began twirling the lethal cutlery over their turbaned heads as they came at Proffit howling like a pair of junkyard dogs.

"Death to American Satan!" those in the immediate vicinity shouted, shaking their fists.

"Kill them!"

"Hack off their genitals!"

Proffit blasted the first Arab in the belly, exploding his intestines in a shower of ketchupy red glop. The second sand-sucker turned tail and scooted for the hills.

A couple score yards, and Z-Comm was out of the throng and on the edge of the plaza. But armed soldiers were now converging on the Z-crew from every direction.

A quick look around showed several large tour buses parked nearby in a large dirt parking area. The crowd attending the rally might have been brought to the plaza by the buses.

A driver of one of the coaches sat behind the wheel, reading an Arabic newspaper.

Cage was up the stairs and had his weapon in the driver's gut.

"Keys," he demanded of the cowering raghead.

The driver shook his head. "No kill, no kill," he said in English. Cage then saw the keys in the ignition. Booting the driver out onto the blacktop, Proffit climbed behind the wheel.

"Ever drive one of these rigs before?" Cage

asked.

"No," Proffit replied. "But like they say, there's always a first time for everything."

Bullets tore sharp, spinning hunks out of the blacktop as the kill contingent of AK-armed troops opened fire on the bus. It screamed across the parking area and crashed through a low perimeter fence to make a bumping, grating entrance onto the highway that fed out onto the desert surrounding the coastal city, throwing up sparks as its undercarriage scraped over the asphalt.

Behind the bus, military vehicles of various types had been hastily pressed into service in a search-and-destroy death run to kayo the escaping bus.

One of the vehicles had a Soviet 7.62-mm RPK machine gun mounted on its roof and its heavy-caliber slugs posed a real threat to the bus.

Cage and Domino again got into sidegunning position, the muzzles of their weapons jutting out of windows shattered with swipes of SMG iron. This time, though, they would conserve their ammo for what was sure to be a one-sided firefight.

The SMGs they packed were no match for the range and power of the 7.62 full-auto weapons that the opposition packed. Add to that the fact that Proffit had only a reserve of a few ammo clips in his rucksack, and Z-Comm's strategy was to outrun, as opposed to out*gun*, the opposition.

Stay alive long enough to reach the LZ for a last-ditch airborne rescue run.

Cage and Domino hit the deck as a salvo of steel-jacketed 7.62-mm tumblers crashed through the rear window of the highballing bus, and sucked the floorboards as the night erupted around them into a vortex of flaming havoc.

BOOK THREE:

Going Ballistic

EIGHTEEN

A Huey Blackhawk and an AH-64 Cobra sat on the desert landing strip at Tarso Ourari, ready for immediate takeoff.

The military insignia on both rotorwing aircraft had been obliterated and the fuselages covered with a special matte black paint that absorbed radar signals, giving them a rudimentary "stealth" capability.

At the controls of the Cobra combat helo sat the Chadian Captain Jahloub with an Army Air Corps lieutenant as his copilot.

The slick driver was Bear MacBeth. Behind him, in military camos and smoking a long, thin cigar, Harry Zabriskie stood behind a GE M134 Minigun. His guns clutching the spade grips of the electrically fired heavy machine gun, Zabriskie made sure that the M134's belt of 7.62-mm steel jackets was properly loaded, and practiced aiming through its pop-up circular pancake sight.

Both MacBeth and the Chadian captain were running through the final systems checks before lifting off into the moonless Saharan night on an emergency covert penetration of Libyan airspace.

Only a short time before, the Chadian outpost's radioman had broken in on Jahloub to report Proffit's distress call.

The captain had notified Zabriskie and Bear, and the helos were immediately rolled from the concealed maintenance bunkers where they had waited in readiness against the possibility of a "hot" extraction from the op zone.

A voice crackled over Bear's headphones.

"All systems read green," the Chadian captain said over the radio link between the two helicraft. "Am taking off on course null-null niner, seven-seven, mark five-zero."

"Roger on that," Bear said back. "Am following right behind you. Out."

The Cobra's turbines screamed into sudden violent action as the smaller but more heavily armed combat aircraft lifted off the landing pad in a swirling cloud of pale desert dust, its tail bobbing from side to side.

It hovered nose-down for a few moments and then, like some animal that had gathered enough strength to spring, suddenly rose straight up to an altitude of 60 feet, swung its nose to the northwest, and moved forward at high speed.

MacBeth gave Zabriskie the thumbs-up and pulled down the twin-tubes of the Litton M927 aviator's night-vision goggles that he would use for navigating the Huey on a covert run where any kind of running light would make them vulnerable to enemy fire.

He pulled back on the collective and the slick immediately soared to cruising altitude as quickly and as smoothly as an express elevator.

The heavier, less agile but more powerful slick got airborne just behind the smaller, armed-to-the-teeth Cobra and joined the combat craft flying-nap-of-the-earth over the shifting sands of the Sahara desert on a long-range rescue mission into the heart of Libyan territory.

Strapped behind the M134 on elastic military webbing, Zabriskie ran a mud check on his monocular NOD. The single-tube nightscope would come into play later on, if and when he was called upon to lay down a Minigun cover blitz to help Z-Comm out of a hot LZ situation. The light-amplification device checked out, and Zabriskie settled back to finishing his smoke while scanning the desert ground passing by below.

In accordance with the prearranged emergency procedure that Z-Comm had established before beginning Cage, Domino, and Proffit's covert penetration of Tripoli, they knew the rough map coordinates of a group of wadis that Proffit would try to steer the team toward.

Five miles from that point, they would be within range of the transponder beacon put out by the compact AN/PRC 112 commo unit Proffit carried. The helos would receive visual confirmation of Z-Comm's position by flares and red signal smoke popped at the LZ.

Sure, there were a lot of ifs in there, but Bear and Zabriskie tried not to think about them as they floated like dark avenging angels above the treacherous sands only a few score feet below them.

Wham! Wham! WHAMMMMMM!

The bus bucked like a mule as mortar strikes tore gaping craters in the blacktop surface of the desert highway. On either side of it, the sands stretched away to distant mountains that stabbed jaggedly into the belly of the starlit desert sky.

Cage and Domino triggered a few bursts of SMG fire, but the mechanized pursuit crew was savvy enough not to get into range of Z-Comm's guns.

They had the firepower and the range in their favor, so why should they run the risk of getting blasted all over the desert? All they had to do was keep throwing deadly heat at the escape vehicle and let the law of averages take care of the rest.

A round in the right place would be all it would take to blow the bus straight to the planet Neptune.

The pursuers had plenty of ammo and all

the time in the world.

This could be a turkey shoot if they played their shit right.

Cage understood this fact about their situation as well as the Libyans did. In the absence of heavier weaponry, Z-Comm would have to try another approach at shaking the opposition off their backs.

The rocky highlands over which the tour bus now traveled would soon give way to low-lying desert country. Cage went up front and told Proffit to stop the coach as soon as they had opened up some distance between the sheik snuff posse and themselves.

While Proffit stomped at the gas, Cage taped together Z-Comm's two C-4 bricks and wired them to a miniature electronic detonator for a 15-second delay and taped the explosive charge to one of the seats located directly above the fuel tank.

Bahhh-LOOOOOM!

The blast violently shook the front end of the bus, lifting its front tires clear off the blasted surface of the desert road. Hissing jets of engine coolant sprayed from the destroyed front end of the bus as a burst of shrapnel razored through the engine and connecting tubes.

Proffit goosed the ignition but the bus was dead in its tracks. End of story.

A mortar round whistled over Z-Comm's heads. A moment later it detonated to one side of the stricken tour bus with a blinding flash and ferocious concussion waves that blew out most of the bus's windows and shook the rocky floor beneath them.

"Okay, last fucking stop!" Cage hollered as he slung the Commando SMG over his shoulder and peered out of the shattered window. "Break for that line of boulders over there. Wait for the bus to blow before we go any further."

Z-Comm hustled out the front and rear doors of the crippled steel leviathan that now completely blocked the ribbon-thin surface of the mountain road.

Dodging a hail of 7.62-mm sizzlers that made the sand leap crazily at their bootheels as though devils were spitting from the bowels of hell, the strike team sprinted for cover on the boulder-strewn slopes of the craggy mountainside.

As they hit the dirt behind a line of boulders, Z-Comm heard the bus go up in a screaming fireball of destruction as a Libyan HE round caught it in the gas tank.

A pulsebeat later, the C-4 pack went up, the secondary joining with the primary blast to give birth to a screaming gusher of flame that shot scores of feet into the Stygian darkness.

In moments, spiraling pieces of flaming shrapnel rained down on the Z-crew as they hunkered behind the limited protection of the boulder field.

All that was now left of the bus was the smoke-wreathed wreckage of its undercarriage, burning like some bizarre funeral pyre.

Bullets whined as they spanged off the boulders that gave Z-Comm tenuous cover from the fast-closing kill squad as the Libyans walked their fire toward their badly outgunned targets.

So far, the boulders shielded them from the rain of 7.62s, but this was at best a stay of execution. A single mortar round would end Z-Comm's mission with ultimate finality.

End it damn soon too.

Using their short-range weapons, Z-Comm returned fire. But the light-caliber rounds cranked out by their SMGs still fell far short of the range and power necessary to do anything more than keep the enemy at bay for an all-too-brief respite.

As soon as their ammo supply ran out—which wouldn't take long—or the moment a lucky mortar round caught them, the fat lady would have sung.

Z-Comm did not and could not know that at that moment the rescue choppers were less than a mile away and closing fast.

They were, in fact, close enough to spot the burning wreckage of the totaled bus. The plume of smoldering debris was as good as a smoke signal leading the rescue team to Z-Comm's position.

"Skyhawk Two to Skyhawk One," Bear radioed the Cobra driver. "I think that's our party down there. Flying over to confirm. Cover my ass. Over."

Bear sharply banked the Huey Blackhawk, screaming low across the mountainside to Z-

Comm's back. He was now able to clearly discern Z-Comm's position behind the line of boulders. To say that it didn't look good was putting it mildly.

"Looks like we showed up just in time to pull their tits from the wringer," he radioed the Chadian Cobra driver. "Going down. Out."

The snake driver rogered Bear's transmission and swung around to position the Cobra to give a sizzling-hot welcome to the Libyan fireteam.

Confusion overcame the Libyans when they spotted the Chadian deathbirds.

The ground crew of Libyans didn't know which directions to turn their weapons. One soldier who was firing a pintle-mounted 7.62 RPK at Z-Comm's position from a Saladian armored car suddenly jerked the machine gun up to fire at the Cobra that was swooping overhead like some mammoth nocturnal bird of prey.

A Hellfire missile streaked from its rack on one of the Cobra's skids and collided with the rear of the Saladin. White-hot splinters shredded through the vehicle's armor and ignited the fuel tank.

The vehicle exploded into a glowing white cloud of vaporized debris that fountained high into the night before cascading back to earth in a pyrotechnic shower.

The tracked APC a few score yards away from it let fly a Frog-7 antiarmor missile at the chopper. The missile—which unlike the

Hellfires the Cobra packed was not laser guided—flew wide of the helo by a mile.

The second Hellfire didn't make the same mistake. It struck the APC dead on, blowing apart its armored chassis as easily as something made of tin.

Its conically shaped warhead produced both enormous blast pressure and temperatures hot enough to instantly liquefy the steel casing of the projectile into a stream of molten metal that squirted into the APC's interior and scrambled the men inside as though they were egg yolks.

Zabriskie blitzed the survivors of the column with a hellstorm of 7.62-mm manrippers that exited the Minigun's muzzle at a mind-boggling 6000 rounds per minute, swinging the M134 to and fro on its pintle mount to inflict devastating casualties on the ground troops scattering in blind panic from the burning remains of the mechanized column.

The one-sided firefight was as brief as it was bloody.

In only a few minutes the Libyan kill brigade had been utterly destroyed. Only smoldering wreckage remained of the armored military vehicles. What the Hellfire strikes hadn't finished off, Zabriskie's Texas twister of 7.62-mm rounds had mopped up with brutal efficiency.

Dead Libyans littered the sands, the corpses lit bizarrely by strobing flashes of light from the guttering wreckage nearby.

By morning, they would provide food for the vultures, lizards, and other scavengers that would swarm in to feast on the gruesome banquet Z-Comm had prepared.

While the Cobra circled the now-silent battlezone, Bear brought the Huey Blackhawk to a perfect landing on the road surface below the rocky mountainside. Z-Comm hustled for the chopper and climbed into the open side hatches. Zabriskie helped each of his battle-weary pards into the chopper's passenger bay.

"Okay, let's get airborne," Cage said, tapping Bear on the shoulder. With the Blackhawk now in the lead, the rescue craft took off from the desert LZ, on a return flight to the covert military base inside Chad, leaving behind a no-man's-land of mass destruction that was buffeted by the hot desert wind.

NINETEEN

The military fax machine whirred softly as the ground station picked up downlinked telemetry from a Keyhole intelsat in high earth orbit transmitting intelligence data from NSA headquarters in Fort Meade, Maryland, to the clandestine hardbase in Northern Chad via the ultrasecret SPINI-COM (Special Intelligence Communications) network.

Page after page of charts, high-resolution photos taken by spy satellites, and intelligence analysis poured into the fax's collation bin. When the print run was complete, the combined data provided Z-Comm with a multifaceted picture of the aftermath of its penetration into the Mad Dog's lair.

The satellite photos made it clear that,

although security had been beefed up at the 'Uqba bin Nafi military base suspected of housing Proteus Chain research and development, massive movement of troops and matériel to protect the installation against attack was not indicated.

From inside Libya itself, reports from intelligence assets on the ground indicated that a policy of damage assessment and control had followed in the wake of Z-Comm's clandestine penetration into Tripoli and the aftermath of the brief but destructive firefight in the desert some 60 miles outside the Libyan capital city.

The intelligence assessment indicated that a willingness on the part of the Libyan Defense Minister to protect his position was at the heart of the puzzling lack of movement on the part of the Libyans.

While the charade that Cage and Domino had perpetrated on the Libyan defense establishment was a source of embarrassment, it had been downplayed by the Moukhabarat as a failed U.S. intelligence penetration that posed few, if any, consequences for the future of the Proteus Chain project.

Coverup fever had broken out among the Libyan power elite.

In fact, the Proteus Chain operation was not even believed to have been compromised by the events which followed Z-Comm's extraction from the Libyan op zone. Refinement and production of the Nazi biologicals were proceeding without delay.

Colonel Daffy himself had expressed a renewed commitment toward a completion date for the deadly cache of CBW agents which he had earmarked for deployment against American targets abroad.

The Libyan loony-toon had presented a comic picture as he ranted and raved inside the camouflaged Bedouin tent outside the El-Azzizya army barracks that served as his office and occasional sleeping quarters, wearing a pair of high-heeled pumps, pancake makeup, and bright red lipstick.

Qaddafi's cross-dressing was largely kept a secret by his cadre of loyal followers. Nobody dared to so much as snicker as the Mad Dog flailed his fists and bellowed that he wanted to see some results fast on his pet project to kill Americans by the millions using the deadly Nazi plague.

While it was apparent to Z-Comm that the Libyan military base at 'Uqba bin Nafi was in fact the site of the Proteus Chain research, there were questions that could not be answered by satellite recon photos or through the often arcane logic of intelligence analysts removed from the nitty-gritty of ground combat in their air-conditioned offices at the CIA's Langley, Virginia, headquarters.

One of those as-yet-unanswered questions that faced Logan Cage as the covert strike team's leader was whether or not the CBW weapons were actually at 'Uqba bin Nafi at all. There was always the remote possibility that the base itself was a deliberate decoy.

Research could conceivably be carried out elsewhere in Libya.

Another disturbing possibility was that duplicates of the Nazi germ-agent cultures might exist at other sites throughout Libya, or worse yet, had even been transferred out of Colonel Daffy's domain.

It was Cage's call.

He was the merc on the ground closest to the action. Cage had the option of calling in an air strike that would annihilate the Libyan germ-warfare research base in a fireball of mass destruction that would send a message to the Mad Dog that even the crown prince of loony-toons could not afford to ignore.

Israeli F16C/D fighter planes armed with TAL-1 terminally guided cluster bombs would carry out a low-profile sweep across the Libyan desert from a hidden runway inside the Chadian border, but the Egyptians would also be in on the mission, albeit playing a less active role.

Their radar crews monitoring the skies over their airspace would be instructed to turn a blind eye toward their monitors during the few minutes the Israeli bombing crews would be engaged in a low-altitude flyover at supersonic speeds.

Like the Israelis, the Egyptians were well aware that a CBW capability on the part of the Libyans was more dangerous to them than even Qaddafi's rumored possession of a nuclear bomb.

The deadly Nazi germ agents that made up the Proteus Chain would be used, that was certain. In some future short and nasty border skirmish of the type that broke out in the Middle East like cases of measles elsewhere, the legacy of the Third Reich's experiments would exact a terrible toll on Egyptian forces.

The Egyptian relationship with Libya had been historically rocky.

Libya was the source of Islamic fundamentalist agitation in that nation's territory, as well as the instigator of the brief but bloody coup attempt that had claimed the life of President Anwar Sadat a decade before. The Egyptian military had agreed to support the clandestine Israeli air strike, as long as no complicity on their own part could ever be proven.

The Israelis, as both the region's pariahs and its most powerful military machine, would be called in to supply the muscle in the blitz on the Libyan hardbase. They had nothing to lose and everything to gain.

But before the go-order would be flashed to send those F16C/Ds screaming across the shifting desert sands on a secret bombing run like avenging furies in the savage night, Z-Comm had one final mission to undertake.

Before annihilation came raining from the skies and the night erupted with the hellfire and thunder of terminal vengeance, the strike team would recross the border from Chad to Libya for a second close-up recce of the target.

Z-Comm would positively confirm or deny the existence of the deadly bugs on the isolated hardbase at 'Uqba bin Nafi.

If they were present there, then the second biggest blast since the biblical cities of Sodom and Gomorrah went up in a pillar of howling destruction would strike the desert like a jagged bolt from the fiery heart of hell.

TWENTY

Under cover of darkness, the Mowag Piranha IS troop carrier slid across the desert sands like some alien insect cruising the dry seas of a distant, hostile world.

The oversized tires and four-wheel drive of the buglike armored vehicle allowed it to glide smoothly across the treacherous surface of the silent desert where ordinary vehicles would have long since become permanently mired.

Bristling with weapons including a turret-mounted .50-caliber MK II machine gun and racks of 40-mm grenade-launchers located forward and aft of the big gun, the Mowag was as formidable a battle wagon as it was a reliable transport vehicle.

Tempered steel plates shielded its front,

sides, and rear, giving it the capability to withstand horizontal fire from NATO 7.62-mm ammo. The armored floor protected combat troops from antipersonnel mines, and the hardened roof from high-explosive-warhead splinters.

Although to the naked eye the pitch black of night made the Mowag practically invisible, state-of-the-art thermal imaging sensors such as Spyglass would see things differently.

Against the background of the cooler sands, the ambient heat of the truck's engine would give it an unmistakable signature to any heat-sensing electronic eyes that might be sweeping the trackless desert wastes on covert sentry duty.

For that reason, the Mowag's metal skin wore a covering of specially formulated chemical foam designed to attenuate the pattern of radiating heat and make it blend into the background, creating an effective thermal camouflage.

Inside their three-ton steel cocoon, Z-Comm rode comfortably in an air-conditioned environment watching the progress of the vehicle through closed-circuit night-imaging TV lit by an infrared searchlight on the Mowag's turret.

Blacksuited for invisible penetration of the enemy base, the shadow warriors carried weapons selected for maximum effectiveness on their clandestine combat run.

Gen III-equipped for nightseeing capability, Z-Comm was ready to stage its covert assault on 'Uqba bin Nafi in the moonless conditions that would give the strike team the critical edge in a surprise infiltration of the Libyan strongbase.

The small, lightweight AUG SMGs the team toted in specially made rigs at chest or thigh were silenced by SIONIC-type noise-suppressors that would quiet the staccato reports of 9-mm autobursts the weapons were chambered to fire. The SIONIC-equipped weapons would give Z-Comm the power to dispatch whispering death to any human targets encountered on the midnight-hour hit-and-git raid.

FRAG, APERS, CN gas, and stun grenades dangling from military webbing insured that Z-Comm's automatic assault weapons would be backed up by deadly antipersonnel munitions.

In addition to its primary armament, the strike team also carried an assortment of other exotic combat gear that would provide a critical safety margin on the blitzkreig run that lay dead ahead.

Air pistols firing tranquilizer darts would be available to deal swiftly with dogs guarding the perimeter fence; a Greener Light Harpoon Gun capable of firing grapnal hooks attached to nylon lines would allow Z-Comm to climb vertically up the sides of buildings like human flies; eight-pound C-4 bricks already wired to timers could be used to soften the base up for the airborne blitz or create diversion as a "force multiplier."

Since Z-Comm's mission on this op would only involve getting positive identification of the Nazi biological cache and not its destruction—which would be carried out by the air strike later that night—Z-Comm carried no high explosives other than the C-4 packs.

The AN/PRC 112 radio Zabriskie toted—a compact descendent of the Vietnam-era rig popularly known as the "Prick 25"—would be used to call in the air strike once the deadly cache of biologicals had been located.

Then Z-Comm would be faced with its greatest challenge of the night: escaping the strike zone with their skins intact.

The Mowag troop carrier deposited the strike team in a small dry wadi less than a mile from the mission zone. Its two-man Chadian crew had orders to wait in the wadi for Z-Comm's return.

If Z-Comm did not return within six hours, they were to radio home base and an aerial strike would automatically commence, sacrificing Cage and his covert warriors in order to blast the 'Uqba bin Nafi base to embers.

With Cage on point, Z-Comm proceeded across the remaining distance toward the base on foot. The night was moonless and the sands radiated heat back in their faces, but a cool breeze wafted in from the nearby mountains.

Somewhere in the desert beyond them as they navigated by compass, Z-Comm heard jackals bay at the black skies. Then, suddenly, beyond a line of high windblown dunes, the base loomed directly in front of them.

Its nucleus was a four-story building of stressed concrete surrounded by single-story blockhouses on every side. A motor pool and guard and radio towers completed the layout. A double row of hurricane fencing surrounded the base, topped by coils of razor-edged concertina wire.

Through their Gen-III light-amplification goggles, Z-Comm could make out the dark shapes of Doberman attack dogs patrolling the narrow runs between the two layers of 20-foot-high perimeter fencing.

Z-Comm waited, probing the strike zone from the cover of the high dunes before deciding on how best to take the target.

Using M976 light-amplifying binoculars with four-power magnification, Cage swept the base until he had a feel for its strengths and weaknesses.

The battery of SAM ground-to-air missiles he had noted on his brief helicopter flyover of the week before would not pose an immediate threat to Z-Comm.

The tracked, mobile launchers would present some serious problems to the F16C/Ds, though, and would have to be neutralized with C-4 charges prior to the Israeli bombing run. Cage mentally scheduled the base's radio tower for demolition as well.

The Libyans would not be given the opportunity to signal for reinforcements.

The low-altitude bombing strike would be quick, clean, and intended to utterly obliterate 'Uqba bin Nafi as completely and as finally as if the earth itself had opened up and swallowed it for eternity.

Cage swept the M976 binoculars across the compound. Guard towers were positioned at only two points, to the north and south. Each tower was equipped with a pintle-mounted 7.62-mm Soviet RPK machine gun and a high-intensity searchlight.

The tower crews were not alert, however. The occupant of one tower seemed to be asleep at his post, while the other carelessly smoked a cigaret, leaning across a railing. Even a novice marksman would have no trouble picking him off with the cigaret flame to sight on.

The base's perimeter defenses were good, but not especially sophisticated.

The 20-foot-high security fence that ran around the base had Y-shaped upper arms supporting its coils of razor-edged concertina wire designed to discourage intruders from climbing over.

Just inside the fence perimeter, security-armored videocams mounted on steel poles backed up the surveillance by the tower crews.

Sure, a good system. But not a great one.

No matter how well placed, no amount of videocams can cover every inch of a secure perimeter, and by that definition, no perimeter can ever be totally "secure."

Cage was able to pick out two operational blind sectors through which Z-Comm could breach the base's perimeter surveillance and penetrate the hardzone undetected.

After a little thought, Cage selected the blind spot nearest the team's position as the point of clandestine entry into the base. He liked it because it would allow Z-Comm to insert at the base's rear, from which the hard crew could fan out to strike a variety of targets at the heart of the Libyan strongbase.

The decision made, black canvas swallowed Cage's night-vision binoculars and he briefly outlined his plan to the rest of the strike team.

In addition to his usual role of floating backup, Proffit would be designated as the sapper on the mission. His responsibility would be to plant the C-4 charges on the radio tower and SAM installation, rendering these useless before the air strike was called down.

Bear and Domino's responsibility would be to secure the radio shack and TV surveillance booth. Cage and Zabriskie would penetrate the main laboratory building to determine if the CBW weapons were present and call in the F16C/Ds if they were found.

Zabriskie's technical know-how would be necessary in the identification of the Proteus Chain cultures.

There was another secondary task for Cage

and Zabriskie.

Kleist, the man who had designed the CBW weapons, was probably on base as well. If he was found, he was to be blown away by whatever method Z-Comm judged most appropriate so that his black expertise would not lead to the duplication of the cache at some other place and time.

Donning night-seeing goggles, Z-Comm moved out from behind the high dunes and silently approached the base's perimeter fence.

The guard dog stood up on its hind legs as the Doberman sighted its human quarry. Its mouth opened and its ears jerked back on its head, although no sound came out of its mouth.

The guard dog had been trained not to make any noise at the approach of intruders. It was only permitted to use its vicious, sickle-shaped teeth to rend and tear. The victim would do all the screaming necessary.

Cage raised the tranquilizer dart gun and fired point-blank into the animal's throat.

There was a soft *pfut*! as the drug-tipped flechette was ejected in a stream of compressed gas.

The tranquilizer dart lodged quivering in the animal's lean, muscular neck.

Moments later, the dog's legs began to buckle and it toppled over on its side, drugged into unconsciousness. The dog would awaken in a few hours, no worse for wear.

If it survived the bombing run, that is.

Wire clippers, Teflon-coated and oiled for silent operation, were produced and cut a man-sized hole in the double row of hurricane fencing. Their noise-suppressed weapons at the ready, the strike team slipped through into the compound beyond.

The nitty was about to turn gritty . . . .

TWENTY ONE

The grappling hooks caught on the edge of the roof and held fast. They were wrapped with three turns of electrical tape, and contact was as silent as it was secure.

Cage and Zabriskie tugged on the lightweight nylon ropes and clambered up the side of the building, black shadows invisible against the indigo sky. An industrial air-conditioning unit supported by I-beams and several large ventilation ducts bulked huge on the gravel-surfaced roof.

Both Z-Commandos went into low crouches near the rooftop's perimeter. Wearing blacksuits and with their faces cammied, Cage and Zabriskie would not be recognizable against the dark backdrop of the horizon as human figures to surveillance from within the compound.

Zabriskie swept the surface of the roof with a field-intensity measuring probe while Cage, his Gen III goggles giving him clear visibility, swept the rooftop with the muzzle of his lightweight AUG 9-mm assault weapon.

When the probe showed no evidence of alarm circuitry on the roof, Cage signed to Zabriskie that they were to enter the building through one of the large ventilation ducts projecting from the rooftop.

The merc penetrators silently removed the upper cowling of the duct and peered along a crawlspace just large enough for a man to shimmy down through.

Shining an infra-red light beam that was invisible to the naked eye down the shaftway —the beam was as good as a flashlight in conjunction with the Gen IIIs—they could observe no obstruction down the length of the crawlspace.

A faint light glimmered a few yards down, probably a ventilation grating that opened onto a room or a corridor down in the building's interior.

While Cage covered Zabriskie with the AUG, the Z-Commando gadgets-whiz eased himself feet-first into the crawlspace.

The ripple soles of Zabriskie's boots touched the bottom of a shaftway that ran perpendiciular to the first duct and passed a grating that gave access onto a brightly lit corridor.

Backing down one side of the shaftway on all fours, Zabriskie wound up with his head pointing toward the grating. He signaled for Cage to follow him down before flattening against the bottom of the crawlspace.

When Cage had maneuvered into position opposite Zabriskie, they both peered through the grating into the corridor beyond.

They could see a security camera positioned at one end of the corridor. They waited until the camera suddenly rotated downward, Domino's signal that the TV surveillance booth had been secured.

The grating was securely bolted to the opening of the ventilation duct. Again, Teflon-coated steel wire cutters were brought into play until the duct was free of obstructing iron mesh.

Beginning a door-to-door search, Cage and Zabriskie quickly established that this area was used for administrative offices of no particular importance to their soft probe of the base.

Turning an L-shaped bend in the corridor, they stumbled on the section housing the research labs. A locked metal firedoor was set in the wall at the corridor's end. Cage gently tapped the walls to either side of the door with the tips of his fingers.

"Drywall," he whispered.

Zabriskie nodded, sweeping the sensor bulb of the field-intensity probe across either side of the door frame. Suddenly, the needle on its VU meter jumped into the red, indicating electrical wires running through the wall.

It was a sure bet that the door was hooked up to an alarm system.

Going into his rucksack, Zabriskie extracted a pneumatic suction device. Crouching, he pressed the black metal hemisphere to the wall in front of him while Cage stood guard. A powerful vacuum clamped the industrial-strength suction cup to the surface of the drywall.

He next took out a battery-operated sawzall and started it up. Encased in Styrofoam, the sawzall emitted a muffled whine as Zabriskie used the all-purpose cutting tool to shear a rectangular section out of the drywall close to the corridor floor. He pulled it free with the pneumatic suction device.

Crawling into the darkened lab, Zabriskie replaced the section of wall behind himself and Cage.

Their Gen III night-seeing goggles revealed that the dark room was filled with cages. The cages contained laboratory specimens of various kinds used for experimental purposes.

The lab animals began gibbering in mindless terror as they sensed the presence of human intruders. Same began clawing frantically at the bars of their tiny prisons.

There was a swing-door to their left that opened onto another, smaller, room. A sign posted beside it read in English, French, and Arabic: *Masks and sterile robes required beyond this point.* Their pulses quickened with the realization that they were about to locate what they had come to find.

Removing the Gen IIIs, donning face masks that would give better protection against chemical and infectious agents than any surgical mask, and switching on flashlights, Cage and Zabriskie passed through the swinging door into the laboratory beyond.

On a table was scientific equipment used in genetic-engineering research. A Zeiss-Nikon microscope sat on a desk beside racks of test tubes, beakers, and other laboratory glassware. A centrifuge containing test tubes stood in the middle of another table along with other experimental implements.

Yanking open a refrigerator door, Zabriskie stood still for a moment before motioning Cage over.

Row upon row of petri dishes used in the culturing of bacteriological agents were inside the refrigerator.

Zabriskie reached inside and picked up one of the circular glass dishes. On its side was written *Pasteuralla Pestis.* It was the Latin name for bubonic plague. Another read *P. Meningococcus,* a strain of spinal meningitis bacteria. Still another, Rocky Mountain spotted fever.

In all, Zabriskie counted 37 strains of deadly germ cultures that were growing inside the hermetically sealed glass dishes filling the refrigerator.

Zabriskie nodded at Cage.

They now had their confirmation of the Proteus Chain.

Without warning the lights came on.

"Turn around," a voice behind them commanded simultaneously. "Turn around very slowly. Any sudden moves and I shoot to kill."

The voice was German-accented.

As their vision cleared, Cage and Zabriskie found themselves staring at a very angry Hans Kleist packing a very large and very lethal automatic pistol.

Flattening against either end of the squat concrete blockhouse which housed the base's radio shack, MacBeth and Domino stole a glance inside through a dirty casement window.

A bored radioman sat with his dust-caked boots propped up on the edge of a steel desk covered with olive-drab racks of military communications equipment as he thumbed through an issue of French *Oui.* More pornographic magazines were stacked on a table nearby, beside a hot plate and a coffee machine.

The Libyan's coal-black eyes were riveted on a centerspread showing a large-breasted Oriental woman with a hirsute vagina and a clitoris that had been Dippity-Do'd until it shone like a 60-watt lightbulb.

Another soldier entered the radio room from a door set in the wall. He stood beside the man in the chair, admiring the split-beaver centerspread. Both Arabs laughed as the first one turned the page.

Bear moved in first as the new arrival went toward the coffee machine and poured himself a cup. As the standing guard saw him, he dropped his coffee cup and grabbed for the Makarov 9-mm automatic holstered at his hip.

Bear's noise-suppressed AUG spit twice and the top of the guard's head exploded silently into a bloody red carnation as brain matter and skull fragments spattered from it in all directions.

Bear's kill pivoted and fell backward across the coffee-making equipment, knocking it to the concrete floor with the cacophony of shattering glass. The Libyan was now beyond enjoying the hot coffee that poured all over his bearded face from the overturned coffeepot.

The soldier boy in the chair dropped his recreational reading and put his hands up. He stared at the two blacksuited commandos with his mouth agape and a stunned look on his swarthy, beard-stippled face.

Bear stooped and picked the porn magazine up off the floor. "Needs a haircut," he said, opening at random to one of the photo spreads. He threw the smut rag into the terrified soldier's lap and disarmed the Arab of his Soviet Bloc automatic pistol.

MacBeth covered Domino while she used a commando knife to hack off a length of electrical cord from one of the radios and used it to hogtie the guard. Then she stuffed him inside a metal locker against one of the cinderblock walls and locked him inside with a hunk of duct tape over his mouth.

Pop! Pop! Pop!

Silenced 9-mm rounds punched holes in the housings of the sensitive electronic equipment in the radio shack, turning the commo units into worthless junk with a minimum of noise and effort.

When they were satisfied that nothing more would be transmitted from the 'Uqba bin Nafi radio shack, Bear and Domino high-tailed it for the rallying point outside the base to await linkage with the rest of the team.

Hans Kleist was a man totally committed to his project. He was near death, but before the Reaper claimed him Kleist would see to it that the lethal weapons he had created almost a half-century before would be unleashed on the Reich's hated enemies.

Kleist was a man obsessed with a delusion. A delusion almost a half-century out of synch with reality.

The Nazi often remained in his laboratory for days on end, taking his meals while working and catnapping on a cot in a small storage room off to one side of the main laboratory complex.

Kleist didn't require much sleep. Except for a few naps here and there, his lifelong amphetamine dependency kept him awake practically around the clock.

He had been lying on his cot when he'd been startled by the soft sounds of intruders into his domain. Stealing from his room, Kleist had been horrified to discover that the ventilation grate was missing from the corridor outside.

Hotfooting it back into the storage room, Kleist had swallowed another speed capsule and returned toting the .45-caliber Sig-Sauer automatic he always kept nearby in case of emergency.

Kleist had stumbled on the two black-suited commandos as they stood in front of the refrigerator examining the petri dishes full of bacterial cultures.

A sadistic smile crossed the Nazi's cadaverous white face. His black pushbutton eyes glittered with a cold, poisonous light. He jerked the Sig in his fist upward to indicate to his prisoners that they should continue to keep their hands in sight.

Cage and Zabriskie did what Kleist ordered them to. He handled the weapon with the precise movements of a man who was no stranger to firearms—and indeed the former Nazi major-general was.

"So you have come to destroy my work, eh?" the Nazi asked. "Who are you? Israelis?" he demanded. "Tell me. I demand to know."

Then Kleist's eyes widened as he suddenly grasped the truth, "No," he answered for himself. "Americans. *Jah, jah. Americanishe schweinhunde!* You are the same commandos who staged a raid on our base in France, *nicht wahr?*"

"Put away the blaster, Kleist," Cage told the Nazi. "It's time to pay the check. The base is targeted. One way or other this place is going to turn into a pile of slag in less time than it takes to bread a schnitzel. We can even pull you out with us. Our primary interest is the Proteus Chain cultures. You're of secondary importance."

The Nazi smiled again, his red-veined patrician nose wrinkling obscenely over the thin, bloodless lips.

"Yes," he returned. "The Proteus agents. Are you aware that Hitler himself commissioned the project? Yet the *sheisskopf* did not give the order to use the destructive power of his bioweapons against the *verfluchter* Allies. He yielded to weaklings who babbled about compromise. In those final days, the Fuhrer was dying of syphilis. It had turned his brain to useless slime."

The Nazi waved Cage and Zabriskie away from the refrigerator, and held them at gunpoint while he reached inside and came up holding a stoppered test tube.

"I want to show you something," he said in his wheezing voice. "Do you see that animal in the cage there?" he asked, hitching his chin at the small rhesus monkey.

When neither Zabriskie or Cage answered, the Nazi shrugged and lifted the cage by its handle, placing it inside a hermetically sealed glass chamber at the center of the room and set the test tube in a rack beside it. Using a remote robot arm, he burst the test tube, exposing its contents to the atmosphere in the chamber.

The frightened rhesus monkey immediately began to erupt with sores all over its body. Its eyes popped out of its face and blood coursed down its fur. Then the rhesus went into terminal convulsions.

It died kicking its legs and thrashing its arms and tail on the floor of the chamber. Kleist hit a button and the sound of a blower was heard as the contaminated atmosphere was pumped from the sealed chamber and vented deep underground.

"Now I want the two of you to step into the chamber," Kleist said. "If you don't, I will kill both of you right now."

Cage turned and began walking toward the death chamber. As he passed Kleist, he suddenly ducked low under the Nazi's outstretched gun hand and jammed his forefinger behind the trigger.

Kleist squeezed but the gun didn't fire. With a twist of his wrist, Cage had wrenched the pistol from the Nazi's hand.

Kleist fell back against a table. His hand groped behind him blindly. His fingers closed around one of the petri dishes of Proteus agents the Z-Commandos had taken from the refrigerator.

The Nazi held up the petri dish and prepared to hurl it at Cage and Zabriskie.

Cage pumped a 9-mm AUG burst into Kleist's belly before he could hurl the deadly germ culture. He and Zabriskie sprinted across the lab and shut the airtight fire door behind them. The amphetamines coursing through Kleist's bloodstream kept the nearly dead man on his feet, even with half his stomach shot away.

Through the double window in the wall they watched with a mixture of horror and fascination as the Nazi thrashed around in mortal agony, knocking over racks of laboratory glassware as the deadly bugs began to work on him.

Whatever Proteus agent was contained within it produced an instantaneous and startling effect.

Kleist's face became soft and began to flow like putty. His features ran like flesh-colored clay and dripped from his skull, revealing the bloody network of muscle tissue and exposed bone structure beneath.

Kleist's pushbutton eyes were still alive in their sockets, though, bugging out hideously as the Nazi screamed at the top of his lungs and pounded away in desperation on the double window. All that was left of his face was gleaming-wet bloody bone. His fingers were now the hooked claws of a skeleton.

But Kleist's screams didn't escape from the soundproofed lab.

The lab had become his tomb.

In minutes it would become his funeral pyre.

TWENTY-TWO

Some premonition of imminent danger had been keeping the Hook up at night. He had taken to walking the base perimeter, conducting his own personal patrol despite the protests of the Libyans.

The former SS Werewolf terrified the Arabs. Eventually, they permitted him to do as he pleased. Armed with a Mauser machine pistol, the Hook roamed the base, patroling wherever and whenever he wanted.

Tonight, as if guided by some unseen premonition, the hulking Nazi discovered Z-Comm's entry point in the perimeter fence almost at once. He spotted the drugged Dobermans a moment later.

The Hook knew immediately that intruders had penetrated the base not too long before, and were probably still inside it.

He also had a good idea of the identity of those intruders.

They could only be the American commandos who had staged the assault on the French warehouse.

If this were true, then the Hook was ready. If not for the blast of air generated by the concussive force of the exploding warehouse that had acted as a natural fire extinguisher, he would have suffered third-degree burns over most of his body.

As it was, the Hook had been severely burned. The doctors had told him that he was lucky to be alive. His face and upper torso had been hideously disfigured. The Hook had refused the skin grafts they'd offered.

What did he need surgery for? He had worn all his combat scars as badges of honor. These new ones would be no exception.

The Nazi had a score to settle with the mercs who had done this to him, though.

Especially with the big one.

The raw, bloodspurting stump that MacBeth had made of his right arm had been refitted with a new prosthesis. This one was bigger, sharper, and deadlier than the hooks he'd worn before.

As though linked by some telephatic umbilical cord of all-consuming hatred, the Hook could now feel the presence of the big, bald American commando who had chopped off his artificial limb. He would make the pigfucker pay ten times over. For MacBeth, the Hook had reserved a special place in hell.

Easing his Mauser from its chest rig, the Hook strode back through the base, and discovered the wreckage of the radio room that Domino and Bear had raked with autofire.

Unable to get the phone to work, the Hook ran outside and pulled open the box housing a security line.

"Imbeciles! The base has been penetrated!" he bellowed into the mouthpiece in pidgin Arabic.

"Place all troops on full alert!"

The watch commander knew better than to argue with the mammoth German. Racking the security phone, he immediately ordered a general alert.

At once sirens began klaxoning all over the base. Libyan troops poured from their barracks as the installation went to full red-alert status. Mauser in hand, the hulking stormtrooper prowled the strongbase like a savage predator thirsting for the blood of his hidden prey.

Turning a corner, Bear and Domino came face-to-face with the hulking Hook. The Nazi's hideously scarred face twitched with profane malice bordering on sexual desire. The cold glass eye at the center of the puckered slash glared with fiery hatred.

Light glinted off the wickedly honed needlepoints of the steel prosthesis. The Hook was now even uglier than before. Layers of scar tissue mutilated both sides of his face, giving him the appearance of some mummified horror who stalked the desert night bent on settling some ancient blood debt.

"I had hoped that it would be you," growled the Hook, training the Mauser on the Z-Commandos as his lips curled into a perverted smile. "But I'm not going to kill you, at least not with this," he added.

The Hook tossed the long-barreled 9-mm autopistol into the dust at his boots. The Mauser dropped to the ground with a dull clatter.

"Man to man," he challenged the big merc. "We fight on the brink of Armageddon. We spill blood in the Twilight of the Gods."

"How about we just flip a quarter," said MacBeth, who had jerked his SMG barrel at the Hook's gut. "I'm in kind of a rush right now."

"Do not mock me," the Hook bellowed in rage. He raised his hand, the hooked prosthesis glinting malevolently. "I could take the woman with me to hell even with a dozen bullets in my gut."

"Okay, Fungus Face," MacBeth returned, handing Domino his AUG SMG. "Just remember that you called it."

Both men circled each other in the dimly lit maintenance building, each looking for an opening. A cruel smile crossed the big German's face as he swiped the steel prosthesis through the air so that light glinted across the deadly sickles on its end. MacBeth knew he had to keep out of the way of those wicked flesh-rippers to stay alive.

Domino kept her silenced AUG trained on the circling combatants, knowing that MacBeth was out of his mind to accept the Nazi Werewolf's demented challenge, but also knowing that there was no way of stopping the Bear once he'd made up his mind to do something—even committing suicide.

The klaxoning sirens announced the imminent meltdown. They had minutes until someone stumbled on them, minutes after that till the air strike blew the base sky high.

The Hook charged MacBeth, and the two giants locked in a deadly embrace. They went down kicking and tussling on the concrete floor.

Both men rolled and grunted until the Nazi maneuvered himself on top of MacBeth. With a loud, crazed bellow, he pulled back his arm and launched a savage, piledriving left into the Bear's jawline.

Blood spurted from MacBeth's face. The Hook's prosthesis gleamed as he raised his steel claw over his head. "Now I'm going to rip off your face," he said in a knife-edged whisper. "So I can have a look at what is underneath."

The Bear pitched a handful of gravel into the Nazi's eyes, temporarily blinding him. The Hook bellowed and reflexively raised his hands to his face.

Bear punched the Nazi in the gut with enough force to send him tumbling off him. Lurching to his feet, Bear launched a savage kick that would have connected with bone-crushing impact against the side of the Werewolf's bald head had not the Hook side-stepped at the last moment.

Grabbing MacBeth's boot, the Hook wrenched for all he was worth and sent MacBeth staggering backwards.

The Hook now whipped a combat knife from a boot scabbard and lunged at MacBeth. His eyes gleamed with a malignant fury as he swished the deadly blade back and forth in slow curliques.

"Genuck mit das kinderspiel," he snarled. "It is time to end the game."

Domino sighted her AUG on him, but Bear waved her off. One way or the other, he was going to take care of the Nazi giant himself.

If the Nazi now wanted to fight with knives, fine, then he'd fight with knives.

Whipping a razor-sharp K-BAR from its sheath on his thigh, MacBeth countered each thrust of the Nazi's prosthetic hooks and glittering blade. The Nazi was doubly dangerous. If the steel claws didn't get Bear, the knife was there a pulsebeat behind them.

Feinting and dodging, bobbing and weaving, both men again circled each other like stone-age predators, each jockeying for an opening through which to strike through to a vital area as the death pavane brought them near a pneumatic fork lift on which a Jeep was raised for maintenance.

The deadlock was broken as the Hook

feinted suddenly to the left and lunged at MacBeth with an underhand stab of his knife. The serrated steel blade sank into the Bear's upper thigh. Blood spurted from the ragged wound, soaking his blacksuit and staining the concrete floor.

As the Nazi drew back to plunge the knife in again, MacBeth dropped to one knee, caught the Nazi's foot, and flipped his opponent over the edge of the fork lift pit directly behind him.

The Hook scrabbled around in the bottom of the refuse-littered trough as MacBeth lunged for the lever that controlled the pneumatic lift.

"Damn you!" cursed the Werewolf as he managed to get his right arm out of the trough. The Hook's gleaming prosthesis grabbed desperately for purchase on the lip of the pit like the head of some bizarre, poisonous snake flushed from its lair.

"Damn you to—"

Throwing it into reverse, MacBeth sent ten thousand pounds worth of steel hammering down on the Nazi, crushing him to pulp in the maintenance trough.

The prosthesis popped loose from the stump it had been attached to and bounced across the floor, rolling past Bear's feet. Bear stopped it rolling beneath the tip of his boot as a hideous shriek rose up from the killing zone below. It was cut short a moment later.

MacBeth stooped and picked up the gleaming artificial hand.

Blood dripped from the hooked steel talons.

"Remember, you called it," Bear said toward the Hook's concrete mausoleum. Then he tossed the grisly war trophy into the shadows, hearing it roll to a stop with a hollow clatter.

Domino threw MacBeth his AUG 9-mm SMG. The two Z-Commandos scrambled out into the compound, throwing fire from their hips at a brace of Libyan troopers who suddenly spotted them.

MacBeth pulled a FRAG grenade from shoulder webbing and lobbed it underhand at the advancing troops. Those who survived the shower of razoring steel splinters were cut down by Domino's AUG blitz of 9-mm fragmentation rounds.

Zabriskie and Cage linked up at the rally point and fought their way toward the base parking lot, where they commandeered an open-top Walid four-by-four and raced toward the main gate, picking up Proffit, Domino, and MacBeth on the way.

Proffit blew the C-4 charges he'd planted everywhere using a remote radio detonator. The radio tower shot toward the moon in a hot shower of pinwheeling flame and buzz-sawing metal fragments. Moments later, the mobile SAM missile-launchers exploded, taking along two huge rubber bladders of diesel fuel stored nearby with them.

Cage climbed behind the Russian RPK machine gun mounted on a stand in the center of the Walid's passenger compartment and poured 7.62 fire at the line of troops in front of the sentry booths as the armored military vehicle crashed through the black-on-yellow striped barricade ahead of the vehicle traps.

The vehicle traps that popped up right behind them caused a multiple crash as they tore through the tires of the pursuing vehicles.

Activating the AN/PRC 112 tactical radio, Zabriskie called in the air strike.

Boogie time was here.

TWENTY-THREE

At the Chadian airstrip at Ouadi Doum, the squad of F16C/D high-performance strike aircraft received clearance to commence a bombing run on the Libyan military installation at 'Uqba bin Nafi.

Only a few minutes before, the pilots had torn open the secret orders which fully briefed them on the specifics of the clandestine air strike against the Libyan bug factory.

For weeks prior to opening the sealed, numerically coded envelopes containing their orders, they had received simulator training for a night sortie on an undesignated priority target.

None but the squadron leader had known the identity or location of the target until minutes before the strike went down.

Colonel Zvi Harvassi had pulled strings and called in markers to lead the airborne blitz on Qaddafi's germ-warfare research center himself.

Unlike in Z-Comm's raid on the Apocalypse Battalion's training camp inside Libya months before, the American commandos would not be allowed to grab all the glory. This time the colonel would take his fair share of the action.

Besides, Harvassi had been on the Israeli fighter strike to take out the nuclear reactor Iraq had been building a few years before at Osirak. His experience would help make this present raid a blitzing success.

The fighters' estimated flight time to the target that was situated just across the common border that Chad shared with Libya was a little over 15 minutes.

The Israeli fighter pilots had each logged the course data into the LANTIRN navigational and battle-management computer systems onboard their aircraft. The Low Altitude Navigation and Targeting Infrared for Night system would give the strike fighters an under-the-weather, autonomous night-navigation and precision weapons-delivery capability against tactical ground targets.

Several weeks' training in flight simulations of the mission had fully prepared the experienced combat pilots for the coming fireworks. Each was a veteran of the covert bombing run that had smashed the Iraqi nuclear reactor at Osirak in 1981.

They were ready to turn in a repeat performance. One that would bring the curtain smashing down on the Mad Dog's death project.

Scudding over the desert on a low, nap-of-the-earth trajectory to avoid detection from side-looking radars, their fuselages painted in a black-and-gray camo pattern, the jets screamed at supersonic velocities across the distance between themselves and the target, deadly silver bullets primed to annihilate a cancerous growth that threatened to infect the free world.

All the pilots would do at this point would be to monitor their tactical display panels. Getting a fix on the target by comparing the real-time terrain to data stored in RAM memory, the LANTIRN navigational computers would take care of the rest.

A few minutes before visual contact was established with 'Uqba bin Nafi, a series of sharp tones in the cockpit alerted the squadron leader to the F16C/Ds' approach.

A pillar of fire rose from the base's destroyed radio tower and from the position of the wreckage, the pilot also realized that the American commando unit that had infiltrated the base had also taken out the mobile SAM launchers.

The Soviet surface-to-air missiles had been a major concern to the pilots, who had anticipated the possibility that the mission would be a suicide run.

The squad leader radioed this new data to the rest of his men as the aerial death squad screamed low on a flight path toward fiery termination.

In the desert hellzone below, Z-Comm poured streams of 7.62-mm autofire at the motorized column of soldiers pursuing them from the targeted death base as the strike team hauled ass through the desert toward the hidden Mowag APC.

Tracers crisscrossed the night as the fast-barreling Walid four-by-four traded fire with the Libyan chase cars behind it. Cage swung the chattering SovBloc RPK back and forth while Domino, Proffit, and MacBeth blasted the scum patrol with a lethal assortment of automatic weapons. At the wheel, Zabriskie drove with a lead foot, grateful for the four-wheel drive that kept the Egyptian-made military vehicle agile and mobile on a treacherous sea of shifting sand.

Each Z-Commando knew that the air strike was no more than scant minutes away. The base would go up in a titanic fireball and every inch of sand within a quarter-mile radius would be fused to glass by the incinerating heat of the inferno.

Z-Comm's surviving the coming holocaust depended on how much distance they could put between themselves and the doomed Libyan germ lab and how well they could take care of the chase crew on their butts.

Suddenly the night erupted with a banshee turbine scream that originated from the line of dunes just up ahead.

The point F16C/D strike aircraft seemed to appear out of the night like some monstrous desert hawk as its camo-patterned underbelly and forward propulsion nacelles passed only a few feet above the roof of the Walid's armored cab.

A pulsebeat later, the point F16C/D was followed by the two jets on its flanks and the final screaming death eagle at the tail-end of the diamond-shaped blitz formation.

As the deafening thunder of the jet turbines receded from them, Z-Comm could see the fiery vapor trails streaming from the jets' rear nacelles.

Cage continued firing the RPK at the stunned Libyans, scoring a hit on the lead staff car that instantly blew it into a ravaging fireball that lit up the desert, revealing the grim tableau of destruction in a series of hellish freeze-frames between the explosion's strobing flickers.

Bear, Domino, and Proffit hefted LAW rocket tubes to their shoulders and blasted the remainder of the Libyan force to hell and gone a few moments later.

Nothing of the chase crew remained but burning wreckage. Not a solitary survivor, not a single vehicle intact.

They had all disappeared into the black eternity to which Z-Comm had sent them in a volley of flashing destruction.

A moment afterward, the night convulsed as the first jet fighter ejected its terminally guided submunitions.

Each of the TAL-1 cluster bombs scattered 270 bomblets capable of fuzing individually over a radius of 570 square feet.

The effect of the aerial bomblet saturation was instantaneous and electrifying.

The combined detonation of thousands of submunitions at various altitudes produced a dome of fire and blast waves that totally engulfed 'Uqba bin Nafi and made the desert shudder as though an earthquake had rocked the arid wilderness to its ancient, stony roots.

Even a mile from ground zero, Z-Comm was almost shaken from its APC as the night lit up with incendiary brilliance in a sudden hammerblow of fiery, all-consuming fury.

A geyser of incandesent flame belched skyward as the multiple detonations merged into a single massive blast wave of awesome destructive power, the cluster of explosions imparting a spin to the blast. The whirling tornado of fire sucked air into its revolving maw. The firestorm howled in the night like some nightmarish apparition from the darkest depths of the human soul.

Metal, steel, concrete, and living human flesh vaporized completely as 'Uqba bin Nafi was annihilated in the high-explosive holocaust. Then there came a final climactic explosion and a ball of searing flame blossomed hideously against the black, unforgiving sky.

The fireball ballooned into the night on a phallic pedestal of churning, rolling flame as the F16C/Ds screamed back in the direction they had come.

Covered with desert dust, the five black-suited American soldiers of fortune stood mesmerized as they stared into the heart of the firestorm that set the night ablaze with the pyrotechnic turmoil of total, final destruction.

Then, out of the raging inferno's heart, four dark specks appeared. At first the drone of the high-performance jet engines was lost amid the thunderous din of the merging eruptions from the disintegrating base.

A moment passed and the black specks grew with the roar of the F16C/Ds' turbines until the jets became screeching birds of fire that passed over the heads of the Z-Commandos on their return crossing of the Libyan desert, a fierce blast of superheated wind gusting in their slipstreams.

The arid wasteland echoed with the supersonic thunder of jet afterburners until the strike aircraft disappeared completely from sight, the sudden desert stillness now broken only by the crackling of flames from the inferno that Z-Comm had left behind.

"This is how it will look," Domino said, flames dancing in her wide blue eyes.

"How what will look?" MacBeth asked,

climbing aboard the Walid while Zabriskie fired up the engine.

"Judgment Day."

"Babe," MacBeth told the woman warrior, "Judgment Day's already come and gone."

"Okay," Cage said as he climbed down from the white-hot RPK and took a seat beside Zabriskie. "Either get out the weenies and marshmallows or let's get the fuck out of here."

Zabriskie threw the four-by-four into gear and began rolling toward the waiting Mowag APC.

Behind Z-Comm, the rubble of a madman's dreams was already turning to brittle ash.